ROCKIN' AROUND THE CHRISTMAS TREE

BREANNA LYNN

ISBN: 978-1-955359-23-8 (ebook)

ISBN: 978-1-955359-24-5 (paperback)

Cover Design by: Mae Harden

Edited by: Happily Editing Anns and VB Proofreads

Printed in United States of America

THIS YEAR, ROCKIN' AROUND THE CHRISTMAS TREE HAS A NEW MEANING.

Evan Andrews is a grinch with a god complex—and unfortunately, the lead singer in the band I just joined. From the second I walked in, he's made it clear he doesn't want me here. Because a privileged princess like me can't possibly be the real deal for a rock band.

But if he really hates me that much… why did he kiss me like he wants to ruin me?

One taste and everything changes. His mouth is fire and filth, and now I can't stop thinking about what else he's capable of with those hands. He says he doesn't want me. The label says he's off-limits. But I've never been good at doing as I'm told —and Evan can no longer claim he doesn't want me.

We can't stand each other. We can't keep our hands off each other. And with every stolen moment backstage, every moan muffled behind dressing room doors, I'm starting to think the real heat this Christmas has nothing to do with the season.

Because good girls get gifts. But this year? I want Evan Andrews unwrapped.

To Megan...happy belated birthday!
To Mom...happy birthday!
Thank you both for your undying support!

PROLOGUE

One would have to be living under a rock to not have seen the now-viral interview featuring beloved Adored Network actress Hollie Berry and Lyle Tucker on *Wake Up LA*.

The country is divided on Berry's reactions to Tucker's questions and her abrupt firing from Adored Network. The girl next door known for her sweet and romantic Christmas movies shocked millions when she loudly proclaimed that she was "claiming her coal" instead of apologizing for her off-brand behavior at a Vegas nightclub.

What does that phrase mean? Why has it become the top trending hashtag on every social media platform? Why has #ClaimYourCoal become the new battle cry of women around the world?

US Daily has received the full video of the interview between Berry and Tucker and has transcribed it below. This includes the un-aired portion where Berry stormed off the set.

Is Berry justified in her actions? Are Adored Network and Tucker? You can decide for yourself.

LYLE TUCKER: Thank you for being on the show. I must say, not everyone can be as beautiful as you, especially after the weekend you had.

HOLLIE BERRY: Thanks for having me! It's great to be here.

LT: The last forty-eight hours for you I'm sure have been a whirlwind. Do you have anything to say regarding your behavior this weekend? Some are saying that your actions may have put you on Santa's naughty list…

HB: (Laughing) The naughty list… It was my best friend's bachelorette party, but the images and videos were taken completely out of context.

LT: Then please, what was the original context? Because from what the world has seen in a video that now has more than three million views, it looks like you were having sex on stage with a male stripper.

HB: Well, that's a little dramatic considering I was fully clothed and he was still in his Tarzan loincloth. There was absolutely no sex involved with our weekend.

LT: Thank you for bringing that up. The selfie of you next to a half-naked man is a little off-brand for you, don't you think? You're the sweetheart of the Adored Network, known for their sweet and romantic movies. What has Adored said to you about your behavior in terms of the video and photo?

HB: The dancer is a fan of my movies. He and his husband watch them every year on the network. He asked for a selfie afterward. I have *never* told a fan no if they want a picture. And as far as the network goes, Adored hasn't said a thing. My private life is mine to do what I want with, as long as it doesn't go against my contract. And attending a dance performance certainly isn't forbidden.

LT: A dance performance? You call men dancing for women in nothing but their underwear a dance performance? Sounds more like a strip club to me.

HB: It wasn't a strip club. Naked Heat is a dance performance. It's not like we were there to throw dollar bills around.

LT: Even so, you had to know that the Adored Network would not be happy with how you are spending your free time.

HB: Well, I think that's kind of the point. It's MY free time. And I wanted to spend MY free time celebrating my best friend's bachelorette party.

LT: Actually, we have a bit of breaking news here. I've just been handed a press release from the Adored Network saying that they are terminating your contract with the network for breaking a morality clause and are canceling your next three movies. What is your reaction to this?

HB: ... Um, obviously I don't know anything about that.

LT: Well, it's true. Viewers at home, you are now seeing a photo of the press release that was just sent out by Adored.

HB: (long pause) I'm sorry, this is the press release? Like they just sent this out without even notifying me first? If that's true, then I guess you'll need to speak to my lawyer. I don't think I should comment on this without—

LT: But Hollie, you have to have some feelings about this? These movies you make for Adored made your career and, frankly, are the only reason people even know who you are. You have to have something to say about this decision?

HB: Yeah, I have some feelings. Pretty specific feelings. If that's an actual press release, I think it's pretty (expletive removed) up that they would do that without contacting me first.

LT: Please, Hollie, watch your tone and words. And of course it's an actual press release. Do you think we would lie to you? We aren't the ones being questioned about our moral standards.

HB: MY moral standards? I've lived in Hollywood for 20 years with a squeaky-clean image. Do you have any idea how hard that is? I don't party; I don't sleep around. I do my job, and I'm good at it. God forbid I go to a bachelorette party! How about your moral standards? You like publicly shaming women for something every man in America has done. How does that line up with your moral compass?

LT: My moral compass isn't being questioned here. I wasn't the one who, as it has been described by numerous media outlets and tabloids, dry humped a man in front of hundreds of other women. What kind of message does that say to other women or young girls who consider you a role model? Is that the kind of moral standard you want to set for them?

HB: Yeah, you know what? It is! If women want to take control of their sexuality, I say go for it! Why do men like you get to decide what's okay? I didn't dry hump anyone in Vegas, but if I had, that would be my choice. You want to know about *my* message to women and girls? Here it is. Go out there and make the world your (expletive deleted). If this puts me on the naughty list then so be it. I'll take all the coal. Hell, I'll proudly claim my coal!

LT: You just lost your biggest contract. You are a viral video. Do you really think encouraging women and girls to, as you said, claim their coal, is the best thing you can do right now?

HB: No. The best thing I can do is this… (muffled noises) I'll show you what claiming my coal looks like, you ignorant… (muffled noises)

At this point in the interview, Hollie Berry removed her microphone. So while we can't know exactly what she said to Mr. Tucker as a parting shot, the middle finger salute she gave him as she stormed off stage was pretty clear.

CHAPTER 1

LILAH

"Call from *Mother*. Answer?" The robotic voice is about as excited as I am about my mother's call.

I roll my eyes. I would think after the third unanswered call, my mother would take the hint. But I can predict what happens if I decline it again.

Another call.

This one probably during the band meeting I'm running late for.

"Yes," I grit out.

"Am I finally important enough to earn a moment of your time?" Her tone tells me exactly how this conversation will go, and I grind my molars together so I can make it through as unscathed as possible.

"Hi, Mom."

"I keep getting your voice mail."

"I'm driving." My response is more of a sigh than words. What is it about her that makes me revert back to a sixteen-year-old?

"If you lived at home, you wouldn't need to drive. Our drivers can take you anywhere in San Francisco."

Which is exactly why I don't *live* in San Francisco.

But I keep that comment to myself.

"I live in LA," I remind her. "And I have a job, remember?"

I was over the moon when I was selected to join Just One Yesterday, and I foolishly thought my family would be excited too.

Wrong.

They told me it was time to give up my little music "hobby" and come back to San Francisco and settle down, a.k.a., marry a junior executive from my parents' company and become a lady who lunches. Like my mother. And my sisters.

Pass. I have zero interest in becoming the fourth—not counting my extended family—Stepford wife in my family. My Aunt Sarah, who is an archaeologist currently living at a site in Montana, is the only other woman to buck the status quo.

"Of course I remember. I'm your mother. I remember all of your hobbies."

"It's not a hobby, it's a job. One I'm good at."

"I sometimes feel like your father and I made a mistake entertaining your interest in music."

Because, according to her, Juilliard is nothing but a hobby. A waste of time and effort.

Do not lose your shit, do not lose your shit. It's not worth it.

Thank god I'm almost to Chris's house. Then I have an excuse to end the call.

Or I could feign terrible cell service. It *is* sketchy a little farther back in the hills. But I'm not going to avoid my problems. I simply try to keep them from getting bigger.

Hence why I pretend to be the daughter my mother wants.

"Was there something you needed, Mother?"

"I'm calling about the holiday."

I avoided Thanksgiving this year. I doubt my luck will hold to escape Christmas.

"Christmas?"

She sighs. "Yes, Lilah. It's not like we celebrate anything else in December."

Fucking ouch. My birthday was last week. Must have slipped her mind.

"What about it?"

"Your father and I are expecting you for our annual party on Christmas Day. I'll have your room readied, and you can spend the week with us. There's someone I'd love—"

"I can't, Mother."

"Can't?"

I swear her slow blink is audible through the phone. Like she doesn't understand why I don't immediately drop everything to do as she says.

"I have plans," I hedge.

I don't. But she doesn't know that.

"What plans? It's Christmas, and we're your family."

"The band is recording all month." Lie number two. "And then we're meeting with the label to discuss the tour that starts this spring."

"Lilah—"

Chris's gate is in sight, and I wave to the guard who lets me through.

"I gotta go, Mom. Bye."

I hang up on her sputtering and pull my car to the side of the road so I can lean my head against the steering wheel.

That won't be the last time Christmas and my "invitation" to come home for the holidays will come up. But I'll take my small reprieve.

Maybe I'll head to Montana to see Aunt Sarah.

The blast of a car horn jars me into an upright position.

Evan's Jeep is behind me, and he flashes his lights like I don't see him.

"Asshole," I mutter to the rearview mirror.

It may be childish, but I keep my foot on the brake. If he can act like a four-year-old, then I will too.

Six months. One hundred and eighty days I've spent dealing with his not-so-veiled hostility. Since the day Chris called to tell me I had the job. No, before that. He barely looked at me during the *audition*. Why he hates me so much is a mystery. I tried getting to know him. Tried being his friend. When that failed, I gave it back as good as I got. No matter what I do, his behavior hasn't changed.

In response to another blast of his horn, I throw my car in reverse, the white lights illuminating the surprised expression on his face.

"Take that."

He shakes his head, peeling out and around my car, then speeding around the first curve and out of sight.

As soon as his taillights fade, my triumph does too. What good did that do? No doubt made him more pissed at me than he was before.

I shift my car into drive and follow Evan, albeit at a much slower speed. He's waiting in the driveway when I pull behind him, but I don't see Finn's motorcycle or Milo's car. At least I'm not the last one here. Had Evan not shot past me at the gate, I would have gotten here first.

"Glad to see you finally made it, princess," he sneers as soon as I open my door.

My fingers itch to flip him off, but instead, I take a deep breath and ignore his taunt.

"Not all of us are speed demons. Is it fun?"

His sneer morphs to confusion. "Is what fun?"

"Paying all that money for speeding tickets."

He barks out a laugh, appreciation softening the hard angles of his face.

Pissed-off Evan is enough to inspire all sorts of fantasies —hell, he still makes the Top 10 Sexy List for Rock Stars after twenty years. But this Evan? Smiling, laughing Evan?

This one makes my knees weak. It opens the door on all sorts of thoughts I shouldn't have since he's an ass 99 percent of the time. I smile, taking a step closer, and his smirk immediately fades into his resting dick face.

With a sigh, I shift back and almost pretend I didn't move closer. Instead, I reach into the back of my car for the large bag I use as a purse.

"You could house a family of seven in your bag, princess."

I shrug but otherwise ignore the comment.

"You could probably feed them for ten years with the money you spent on it." His taunt pulls me up short.

"How do you know how much my bag cost?"

"I don't. But that shiny little emblem on the front of your brand-new Mercedes tells me you have money, princess. And lots of it. Daddy's? Seems unlikely that a *struggling musician* could afford it."

My parents come from money, but I don't touch it—most of it will sit in a trust until I get married. Instead, my Aunt Sarah set up a different trust for me. One I gained access to when I turned twenty-five. And I used her financial manager after I got access. The hyper blue metallic Mercedes is a reminder that in a world of black and silver, I'm bright blue and proud of it.

"Eat a bag of dicks, Andrews. I don't answer to anyone, including your self-righteous ass."

The roar of a motorcycle echoes down the driveway in the silence after my outburst, and I use that as my excuse to slam my car doors and head for Chris's house, giving the dick in the driveway as much space as I can.

Screw Evan Andrews.
And not in the fun sense of the word either.

CHAPTER 2

EVAN

*L*ilah Stevens has no idea how badly I want to screw her.

In every position, as many times as possible. All the fucking time.

I wait until she passes me to turn my head. Her hips sway in a siren's call, and my hands itch to press against her curves and take them for a ride.

But I won't. I can't.

First, she reminds me way too much of my ex-girlfriend. The one I found in bed with Milo hours after I broke up with her. Same long blond hair, same wide-set eyes—although Taylor's were blue instead of hazel. Second, and probably the more important reason, there is a clause in our contract with Cornerstone—band members are forbidden to date one another. No fraternization.

What the hell does that mean? Until recently, Just One Yesterday was comprised of five friends from high school. Why is that clause necessary?

The answer to my question pulls up on his motorcycle and kicks the stand down behind my car.

Milo.

Why have we been explicitly told that all employees at Cornerstone were off-limits?

Milo.

Maybe I should hate him for what happened with Taylor. When I found the two of them in bed together the morning after I broke up with her, the black eye I gave him had felt justified. A part of me still feels like my reaction was okay. But after twenty-two years of friendship, I can't write him off entirely. Especially after someone at the bar told Chris they were paid to roofie Milo. By Taylor.

I don't hate Milo for that. But I hate Lilah for making me want her.

I am fucked-up.

Milo kicks off the bike and unclips his helmet. He runs a hand through his hair, shooting me a grin.

"I realize I'm a sexy beast, but it's been a while since you looked at me like that, Ev." He blows me a kiss.

I groan. "You're an idiot."

"It's why you love me, boo."

"Jesus Christ," I say with a roll of my eyes. "Any sign of Finn?"

He shrugs. "He left his house when I did. Should be here any minute. Lilah's here?"

My vision shouldn't turn red at the way he says her name, at the way he gestures to her car. But shouldn't and don't are two different things.

"Yeah."

"Were you a dick to her again?"

"No."

Milo raises an eyebrow and keeps his gaze steady on me.

"Maybe," I correct.

"Ev."

"She started it."

He scoffs. "Yeah, okay."

"Are you two coming inside?" Chris barks at us from the front door.

"We're waiting on Finn."

Finn's Tesla pulls silently into the driveway.

"You were saying?" Chris turns and leaves the door open for the three of us to follow.

I turn, ready to follow, when Milo calls my name.

"Ev."

"What?"

"Don't be a grinch. It's Christmas."

"I'm not being a grinch."

I stalk inside, barely making it past the door when Chris's five-year-old son, Gage, rushes to me and wraps his arms around my legs.

"Evan! Guess what!"

"What's up, buddy?" I lift him and hold him upside down, smiling at his giggles.

"Santa's coming soon."

"He is? Are you sure?" I let him slip a little, and he shrieks another giggle.

"Uh-huh. And I'm on the nice list. Mommy said so."

"Mommy said what?" Chris's wife, Jessie, says as she comes down the stairs.

"I'm on Santa's nice list," he repeats.

"Only if you do what you're supposed to do. Which is what?" She perches both hands on her hips and gives Gage the mom look.

"Evan! Put me down." He squirms to get free. "I gotta go take my bath before I end up on the naughty list."

I flip him right side up, and he races up the stairs, already stripping out of his T-shirt.

Jessie shakes her head with a laugh.

"Lilah's out back."

"Where's Chris?" I'd rather avoid being alone with Lilah.

"Grabbing drinks."

"Correction. Chris is here. Cursing how fucking slow Milo and Finn are." My best friend brushes a kiss on his wife's shoulder.

The front door opens, and the two saunter in like they have all the time in the world. Like they aren't late.

"Have fun." Jessie winks and kisses Chris's cheek. "I'm going to go make sure our son scrubs the pool out of his hair."

Chris doesn't move until Jessie disappears at the top of the stairs.

"Are we meeting in here so Chris can stare at his wife?" Milo jokes.

Chris flips him off without shifting his attention.

"Leave him alone, Milo. He's only been married three months," I say. "Lilah's out back."

Milo rushes to the back door, and I grind my teeth and follow him, leaving Finn and Chris to bring up the rear.

"Lil!" Milo tackles Lilah in her chair and sits in her lap. "Long time no see."

"You saw me yesterday."

Yesterday? Why the fuck did she see him yesterday?

"You two have some sort of extracurricular activity going on? Milo, do I need to pull out the contract?" I spit out before I can stop myself.

"Something in our contract specifically states that band members can't go shopping together?" Milo glares at me, and guilt pricks almost immediately.

"Give it a fucking rest, Ev." Finn claps me on the back and moves around me before pulling Milo off Lilah and dragging him to the couch.

"Sorry," I mutter. The word sticks in my throat.

"Ouch, sounds like that hurt." Lilah pouts her lower lip, and the urge to nip at the plump flesh battles for freedom.

Fuck.

I open my mouth to retort, but Chris whistles loudly behind me, pulling my attention from her.

"Jesus Christ, I'm a fucking babysitter. Ev, sit down. And if you and Lilah can't be nice to each other, then don't say any-fucking-thing at all."

"Jessie's influence?" Finn asks Milo.

"Does she say fuck?" Milo asks.

"*Enough.* I'd appreciate it if this meeting didn't take all goddamn night. I promised my wife I'd help put our son to bed so we can watch a movie together."

"Is that code for—"

"Milo, if you finish that fucking sentence, I'm going to drown your ass in the pool." Chris glares at our drummer.

He holds his hands up in surrender. "I'm done."

"Are you sure?"

Milo taps his finger to his lips as he considers the question before finally answering. "Yeah, that's all I got."

"Good. Now that the comedic portion of the evening is over, I wanted to talk about an opportunity we've been presented with. To perform at a charity concert between now and Christmas."

Finn groans. "Christmas songs?"

"What's the charity?" Lilah asks.

"Santa's Helpers." Chris's glance in my direction is so quick I almost miss it.

It's a charity I'm familiar with. Only my experience was on the receiving end. The charity helps make sure kids from low-income families experience a special Christmas, even if their parents can't afford it.

I give my head a slight shake to assure him I'm fine with

it. More than fine. It's a great chance to give back to the organization that helped my family when I was younger.

"When's the concert?" I clear my throat to get rid of the rasp of emotion in my voice.

"Next weekend. In San Francisco."

Lilah's eyes widen. "San Francisco?"

"Problem, princess?" I can't help but goad.

She glares at me. "No. No problem."

"Cornerstone okay with it?" I ask Chris.

Since Noah left the band six months ago, our label has become a massive pain in the ass. Might have something to do with Noah's departure after a fuck ton of publicity surrounding his overdose.

"Marcus is the one who called me."

I'm not a fan of our label rep. But Chris has to put up with him more than the rest of us. And lately, the interactions have involved more and more bullshit, with zero signs of letting up. After twenty years, we should hold a little more control over our lives.

Not according to Marcus.

"So are we doing the concert?" Finn asks.

"That's why I called you all here. Cornerstone is letting us decide. What do you think?"

"What do *you* think?" I ask Chris.

"I think we should do it. It will be our first concert since…"

Since Noah left.

Since Lilah.

"Me too," Milo pipes up.

"Fuck yes." Finn fist-bumps Milo.

"Lilah?" Chris turns his attention to her.

She studies me for several moments. Like for some reason her answer hinges on mine.

"Yeah, okay. Let's do it," she says.

I'm already outvoted, but Chris still shifts his gaze to me. "Ev?"

With a sigh, I nod. "Fine."

We'll have to pop this cherry at some point.

CHAPTER 3

LILAH

"*L*il, wanna grab a drink with Finn and me?" Milo loops his arm around my neck as we head for the door.

While we nailed down the details of the charity concert, I debated whether to tell my family about my upcoming trip to San Francisco. A major part of me says *hell no*, but there's a small piece—the one still craving their acceptance—that thinks I should invite them to the event. Let them see what I do, why I do it. Maybe then they'll understand.

Keep dreaming, Lilah.

"Umm…"

I've gone out with Finn and Milo a few times, but I've discovered that their number one goal is to find a hookup for the night. Nights like that were fine when I was in my twenties.

But now? No thanks.

That scene hasn't interested me in the last couple of years. Since right around the time I turned thirty, I guess.

Milo pouts his lower lip out. "Please?"

I laugh and push him away. "You know your puppy-dog

look doesn't work on me. You guys go. Enjoy. I need to ask Jessie something."

"You do?" Jessie walks down the stairs, stopping near me. "What's up?"

"Bye, Milo." I wave and wait until he shrugs and closes the front door behind him. Then I turn to Jessie. "Are you going to the concert next weekend?"

How is it already next weekend?

Jessie's face lights up, and she nods. "I am. I've never seen the guys live. And Chris's mom and dad are keeping Gage for the weekend. This is our first weekend away since—are you okay?"

My smile is shaky. "That's my hometown."

"I'd say that's great, but based on the look on your face, I think my assumption is wrong." She tugs me out of the entryway and into the living room.

I shrug. "My family—I'm not sure. It's…complicated."

Jessie's eyes go soft and she puts a gentle hand on my arm. "I'm sorry. Is there anything I can do? Maybe we can make plans as a group."

"Maybe. In a way, I'm excited, I guess. It's my first concert with the band, but…"

Family. Holidays. Arguing with Evan. It's all taking a toll.

"Don't worry. It'll be fun. I'll look at stuff we can do while we're there."

"Thanks."

"Angel?" Chris pokes his head into the room, his eyes widening when he sees me with Jessie. "Lilah, I thought you went with Milo and Finn."

"No. My only plans tonight involve my couch. Good-night. Thanks, Jess."

I flip Evan's car the bird before sliding into my driver's seat. Time for a hot bath, a glass of wine, and my favorite Hollie Berry movie, *All Snowed Inn*. Her Christmas movies are the only reason I keep my subscription going for the Adored Network now that I'm too busy to watch TV.

Too focused on *finally* relaxing, I don't notice my car is significantly harder to turn than it should be until I've made several turns down Chris's ridiculous driveway. I lower the radio's volume, catching the steady thump just as a warning light on my dash illuminates.

"Fuck. Now what?" With a sigh, I pull to the side of the road and step out into the darkness. With a flick of my finger, I activate the light on my phone.

It doesn't take long to find the culprit. My rear driver's-side tire sits on a flat line of rubber.

Headlights wash over the area behind me, and Evan's Jeep rolls to a stop, spotlighting the offending tire. Even in the shadows, his open mouth is clearly visible.

I hold up a hand. "You can just keep your snarky-ass comment to yourself."

I sink my teeth into my bottom lip to stop the irrational trembling, chalking up the desire to cry to being mentally exhausted after dealing with both my mother and Evan.

He stills, studying me silently until the lines of his face relax. My shoulders mimic the release.

"What happened?"

I shrug. "It was fine when I got here."

I think.

"Do you have a spare?"

"You're going to change my tire?" I bite back before thinking better of it.

What can I say? With him, the retorts have become habit.

A muscle tics in his jaw, but he doesn't fire back.

Guilt pinching at my conscience, I sigh. "Sorry. That was bitchy."

"Where's your spare? The back?" He closes the distance to my trunk, and I reluctantly join him.

This close, his cologne is overwhelming intoxication.

At least, that's what I tell myself when I take a second deep breath and release it. He unlatches the trunk, and we stare at smooth, black fabric. No sign of a spare anywhere.

"Fuck," he breathes out. "Maybe underneath."

Without waiting for a response, probably because the words are more for himself than for me, he lowers to a crouch and peers under the car. I try to ignore the way threadbare denim cups his ass like a lover. I do. But over-looking the glorious view in front of me is virtually impossi-ble. The back of his gray shirt rides up, exposing a thin strip of tanned, toned skin, and my fingers prickle with the need to touch.

With a strangled sound, I spin away, blinding myself in the headlights of his Jeep.

"What's the matter?" He jumps up, glancing around.

"What?"

"You sounded like a dying duck."

"What does a dying duck sound like?" I say, propping my hands on my hips with a glare.

"Like you." His lips twitch into a smile, and mine follow suit, my irritation skittering away.

Staying angry with him is safer. Especially in the quiet darkness surrounding us.

But holding on to it is like holding on to waves on the beach.

"You don't have a spare," he says.

"What?"

I bend at the waist and squint into the darkness under my car. "Why would they sell brand-new cars without spare tires?"

He shrugs. "No idea."

"Shit." I pull my phone out of my pocket. The light is still on, and the battery indicator signals it's woefully in need of charging.

"Can I borrow your phone? Mine's almost dead."

"For a tow truck?"

"Roadside assistance, but yeah."

He shakes his head. "It'll be easier to grab someone in the morning. I'll give you a lift home."

"We live in opposite directions."

Evan lives even deeper in the hills than Chris does, and my condo is downtown.

"Who else can you call? Milo?" His jaw locks as he grinds out the name.

What does he care who I call?

"I'll grab an Uber or something."

"Do you seriously not want to be around me so badly that you'll pay for a ride when I'm freely offering?" He steps closer as he speaks, his chest brushing mine in the shadowy light.

"N-no."

I don't trust myself not to kiss you.

"Either take the ride or not, princess. I'm leaving."

He turns on his heel, and my phone chooses that moment to go dark.

"Wait. Let me grab my stuff and turn off my car."

He doesn't turn around, but he nods once.

I rush to grab my bag and push the ignition button. The hum of my engine quiets, and I gulp in the silence.

What the hell am I getting myself into?

I'll just walk back to Chris and Jessie's. It's not that far. I'm in their driveway, for pity's sake.

"Are you coming?" Evan's voice echoes in the silence around us. His engine idling in the background emphasizes the roughness of his voice and sends a shiver of awareness down my spine.

No. No. No. No. No.

"Yes." My voice is breathy, so I clear my throat and repeat myself louder so he can hear me. "Yes."

I've never ridden with Evan. Even when we've gone from one place to another at the same time. Milo, Finn, and Chris, sure. But the pristine condition of Evan's car surprises me. I thought I was meticulous.

"Is this a new car?"

He looks up from his phone. "I've had it about a year."

It looks brand new. The smell of leather mixing with the spice of his cologne is a strange but strong aphrodisiac.

"I sent a text to Chris in case he or Jessie see your car."

He puts his phone on the stand and drives past my Mercedes, taking the curves slower than he took them coming in. The phone chimes, his Bluetooth automatically reading the text.

"From Chris. *Try to be nice.*"

"Goddamn it. I'm *being* nice," he grumbles.

"You are. I appreciate the ride." I almost ask what he expects in return.

Nothing is free.

But I don't want to spoil this tentative peace between us. After battling for the last six months, the lack of bickering is a breath of fresh air. I lean against the door and study Evan in the lights from the dash. His hair is mussed like a girl just ran her fingers through it, and I fight the prick of jealousy. It wasn't a girl. It was probably him. That's one of his anxiety moves—running his hands through his hair repeatedly.

I can't help but fixate on the strong jaw covered in a day's growth and the angular nose that shouldn't add to his appeal but does anyway.

"Do I have something on my face?"

"Huh?"

His lips quirk, and a small dimple pops on his cheek.

What would the softness of his mouth feel like in contrast to the scruff surrounding it?

"You're staring."

Shit. Busted.

"Umm…"

"So, do I? Have something on my face?"

"N-no." I fidget in my seat until I'm focused on the road ahead of us. We're a lot closer to my condo than I realized. "You remember where I live?"

The guys have been to my condo once. It was right after I signed with the band, and we all had swung by so I could change before a fancy celebration dinner.

"We used to live in a building around the block. When we were first starting out."

For a split second, I wonder if he remembers because he thinks about me the way I think about him. But his explanation makes sense and breaks the building bubble of excitement before it can grow too big.

"Oh."

I'm angry. But not at him. At myself. I need a break. Before I have a mental breakdown.

Hollie Berry is calling my name.

He's silent again, and I stare out the window, my fingers on the handle as soon as my building comes into view.

"Thanks for the ride." I should sound more grateful, but at this point, I need to get out of this car.

"Hold on," he says, wrapping long, slender fingers around my upper arm when I open the door. "What the fuck is your problem?" His brow is furrowed, his lips turned down in a frown.

"Not a damn thing." I yank my arm out of his grip. "See ya later."

I'm out of the car before he can respond, but his car door echoes mine. I'm already at the entrance of my apartment building, fingers tugging at the handle, when he slams a hand on the glass, preventing my escape.

"Lilah."

Goose bumps erupt where his breath blows against my neck.

Steeling my shoulders doesn't help. Not with the warmth of him at my back.

I release the door handle, dropping my arms to my sides in defeat.

He turns me to face him, his fingers gentle on my shoulders. His blue eyes search mine, like he can see through the snark and bickering I choose to hide behind. It leaves me exposed. Vulnerable.

"What?" The word comes out on a gasp as he presses me between his hard body and the door, his chest heaving against me, one leg all but wedged between mine.

"Why are you upset?"

"I'm not."

Deny, deny, deny.

"You are."

"It has nothing to do with you."

It has everything to do with him. Or rather, how he makes me feel when I'm not pissed off at him.

One thick eyebrow arches as he studies me.

"I don't believe you."

"Believe what you want." I try to pull away, but since his body pins me to the door, I can't escape.

If possible, he moves closer, and I swear his heartbeat matches rhythm with mine.

"I believe we're both lying."

"Both?" I'm confused.

"You won't admit you're mad at me—"

"I'm not."

He ignores my interruption.

"And I lied to you about why I remember where you live."

The breath catches in my throat at his admission, and I swallow slowly.

"You did?"

He nods and lifts his hand, almost in slow motion, and trails a finger along my jaw. I close my eyes and lean into the warmth.

"I remember everything about you. You're stuck in here."

When I open my eyes, I find him pointing to his temple.

"Because you hate me."

His chuckle is sad. "It would be easier to hate you."

"Easier for what?" I whisper.

"To ignore how badly I want to kiss you."

I loop my arms around his neck and tug until our lips are millimeters apart.

"So do it already," I say on an exhale, reveling in the way our breaths mingle.

Fire blazes to life in his eyes, and a responding throb pulses in my core.

"Lilah." My name is a groan on his lips.

"If you won't do it, I will."

I skim my lips along his once, twice, before he takes control. His tongue surges past my lips to tangle with mine while he shifts his hands to my hips in an almost painful grip. The entire world explodes in bright lights and fire at the way his taste invades my senses. I tangle my fingers in his hair, scratching my nails along his scalp, pulling a guttural moan from him. His erection rests against my stomach, tempting me closer, even though no space exists between us.

A knock sounds against the glass behind us, and we jump apart like guilty teenagers and step to the side to allow the woman to exit. How did one brush of his lips against mine make me forget we were standing in front of the door to my building?

"That was hot," she tells the two of us without breaking stride.

I don't disagree.

My lips still tingle, ready for more, and I look at Evan after the woman turns to leave.

"Do you want to—"

"I should go," he interrupts. "Let me know if you need a lift to your car tomorrow."

He's down the steps and back into his Jeep before I can respond.

What the hell was that?

"Men," I mutter and step inside the lobby.

One man in particular.

Evan Andrews.

Can't kiss him. Can't stop thinking about how his lips so easily mastered mine.

He's an enigma. One I'm too tired to deal with tonight.

Time for Hollie Berry. At least her movies end with a happily ever after.

CHAPTER 4

LILAH

$\mathcal{M}$y lips still tingle with the phantom pressure of Evan's as I lower myself into the steamy, fragrant water thirty minutes later. I'm not sure whether I hate him more for kissing me or for stopping.

"Ugh." Leaning my head back against the tub, I squeeze my eyes shut in a desperate attempt to remove the memories from my brain. "Forget it, Lilah. Focus on the plan."

The plan consists of the glass of wine resting on the shelf stretching across my bathtub, my tablet, and as many Hollie Berry movies as I can watch until I can't keep my eyes open. The plan does *not* include thoughts of Evan Andrews.

Pulling up the Adored app, I click on my watch list, confused when none of Hollie's movies show up.

"What the…?" The other movies I've added are there, but not any of my favorites.

Clicking out of my list, I type *Head to Mistletoe*.

Content not available.

All Snowed Inn.

Content not available.

Chasing Snowflakes.

Content not available.

"What in the actual eff?" I mutter, closing out of the app and tapping on my internet browser.

A search for Hollie's name pulls up a slew of links, and they all say the same thing.

Adored Network severs ties with Hollie Berry over morality concerns.

Adored Network not happy with Hollie.

Hollie Berry storms off set.

The only headline not related to this apparent scandal takes me to Hollie's website, where a hashtag takes over the entire banner.

#claimyourcoal

The more I read, the more I love. Empowering women to be themselves because, as the line she quotes from Laurel Thatcher Ulrich says, "Well-behaved women seldom make history."

If only my mother or sisters would read this.

I snort. Not like they would understand.

The more I think about it, the more I love the idea.

After tonight's kiss, I'm tired of ignoring the attraction between Evan and me. Of being well-behaved. What good does it do me anyway? A never-ending argument with a man who, with only one kiss, obliterated every wall I've built over the last six months.

Grabbing my phone, I pull up Evan's contact.

Thanks again for the ride tonight.

He doesn't respond right away, and I'm halfway through a different movie on a different service—screw Adored Network—when my phone buzzes.

EVAN

You're welcome.

> We have a planning meeting at the studio tomorrow, right?

Yeah.

You need a ride?

Perfect. I didn't even need to ask.

> Would you mind?

You can't ask one of the others?

I hold back the retort burning at the tips of my fingers, begging to be unleashed.

> I suppose I could check with Chris if it's too much trouble for you.

...

The three dots appear and disappear several times. A giggle bubbles up when I picture him typing several responses, that grumpy face on display, before deleting one after another until he finally hits Send.

Never mind. I'll pick you up at 2.

Don't make me wait.

> I'll be on time.

> I promise.

Time for me to claim my coal in the shape of a six-foot-two broody musician.

🎹 🎹 🎹

I'm leaning against the doorway when Evan pulls up in his Jeep. My car has officially been towed and is getting a new tire thanks to Jessie, who stopped by to grab my keys from me this morning and met the tow truck driver. I felt bad at first, thinking she was making a special trip, but she told me she was in town anyway. Without the guilt—and the need to meet a tow truck driver at my car—it left me ample time to get ready for the planning meeting this afternoon.

Ordinarily, my wardrobe consists of ripped jeans and comfy shirts. But not today. No, today I opt for a cropped shirt that reveals a wide strip of skin between it and my fitted leather pants. And my choices pay off. As soon as I open the passenger door, Evan's entire body freezes. I can't see his eyes—damn the mirrored aviators—but the tension in his chest and shoulders is hard to ignore.

"Thanks for picking me up." I rest my hand on his arm briefly. An innocent touch.

With a not-so-innocent intent.

"Like you gave me a choice, princess," he mutters.

"I asked if you minded."

"And when I suggested you check with someone else, you threatened to ask Chris."

"Threat? How is asking our bandmate for a ride threatening?"

"Because you know he told us to get along," he grinds out through gritted teeth.

"Who else should I have asked? Jesus, untwist your panties."

"Milo? Finn? We have two other band members."

"Fine. Next time I'll ask them." What a dick. What the hell was I thinking? "In fact, why don't you let me out? I'll get myself to the fucking meeting."

One hand on the door, I'm ready to exit the asshole's car as quickly as possible.

"I'm taking you, aren't I?"

"Could you be any more of a douche about it? Don't do me any favors or anything."

He opens his mouth like he wants to retort, shakes his head, and closes it again, his teeth clacking with the force. Instead of arguing, he reaches over and practically punches the button to turn on the radio.

Fine. I didn't want to talk to him anyway.

We don't say another word to each other the entire way to the studio and all the way to the conference room where Chris, Finn, Milo, and Chloe wait. Chloe is the new publicist Cornerstone brought on about the time I joined the band. She's relatively young—not quite thirty—and the only time I've worked with her was on some introductory publicity welcoming me to the band. She's deep in conversation with Chris about something while Milo watches her, so obviously crushing, it might be funny.

If I wasn't so pissed off at the asshole who slumps in the chair next to where Finn is scrolling on his phone.

With a sigh I choose a seat on the other side of Finn, capturing Milo's attention.

"What's the matter, Lil?" His attention shifts from Chloe to me.

"Nothing. I'm fine."

He scrutinizes me for several moments, his lips pursed, before shaking his head.

"Nope, not buying. Spill the tea, girl. Tell Uncle Milo why your frown is bigger than Evan's attitude."

A smile pulls at my lips while Evan flips Milo off and Milo returns the gesture.

"Uncle Milo?" I ask.

He nods. "That's me. Listener of all problems and doler-out of awesome advice."

"Does anyone ever listen to your advice?" Evan snarks.

Milo shrugs, a smirk playing on his lips. "Not my problem if they don't. I give great advice. Lilah will listen."

"I don't need any of your no-doubt-incredible advice, Milo," I say.

"How about we talk about the concert then, princess?"

"Andrews, if you ever pull that stick out of your—"

God, what is it about that man that pushes my buttons?

"Okay, Chloe and I think we have a plan lined out," Chris interrupts with a roll of his eyes.

We all stop and look at Chris, except for Milo, who gazes at Chloe like she hung the stars. I peek over at Evan around Finn's back, turning my head just enough to see him out of the corner of my eye. He's the picture of cavalier, and I toss the whole idea of claiming my coal out the window. The kiss last night was obviously a mistake.

It's more than clear exactly how indifferent he is to me.

Shaking my head, I focus on Chris.

"We're going to head up the day before the concert—"

"Flying?" Finn asks.

"Driving. Let's try to arrive under the radar to avoid a mob," Chris clarifies.

"The day of the concert, a local radio station is hosting Chris for an interview, but otherwise you'll have plenty of time for sound check," Chloe says.

"We're the last band of the night," Chris tells us. "So after we're done, we can head back to the hotel."

And as quickly as it began, the meeting ends, everyone filtering out of the conference room before Chloe calls me back at the last minute.

"Lilah?"

"Yeah?" I turn back to face the young woman, my hand falling from the door.

"What are your thoughts on endorsements? Chris has done a few in the past, but a couple of companies reached out to see if you'd be interested. They like the idea of a female rocker."

Really?" There are hundreds of other female rock stars or pop stars in LA. Hell, Michaela King's latest single is sitting in the top three on the charts and has been for months.

She nods. "Nothing crazy. A keyboard company and a makeup rep have reached out, and I'm still going through other offers. Interested?"

I shrug. "Maybe? Can we talk about which ones? Maybe you'll have some recommendations after going through them?"

Chloe's face brightens. "I can totally do that. I'll let you know after the concert next week."

"Thanks, Chloe. Have you…"

I want to ask her if she's aware of Milo's crush on her, but really, it's none of my business.

"Have I?"

"Have you…ever been to San Francisco?"

"I went to college at Berkeley, yeah."

"Are you going to the concert?"

"Marcus hasn't said. Do you think I should?"

I nod. "Yeah. It'll be fun. A good way for you to get to know everyone." Like Milo. "If nothing else, you can show me some of your favorite haunts."

"Aren't you from San Francisco? I thought I read that somewhere."

"I haven't lived there since I was a kid."

Before I escaped to my favorite place in the world.

Juilliard.

Where my mother and sisters' focus didn't extend. Where

Aunt Sarah visited me for the holidays and we formed our own family traditions.

"Oh."

"What do you say? Will you show me around? Jessie's supposed to come too. Maybe we can all hang out."

She smiles at me. "I'd like that."

"We'll work out the details later. I need to pick my car up from the shop, but think about where we should go."

"Okay."

I wave my goodbye and head out into the lobby, hoping to catch a ride with Milo or maybe Finn if they haven't taken off already. I stop short when I find Evan leaning against the wall in a cocky pose.

"Need a lift?"

"Not from you."

"Your car isn't here." He says it like I'm not already aware of that fact.

"What do you care, Andrews?"

I head for the elevator, irritated when he follows.

"I brought you here."

Like that's an explanation. Or a reason to subject myself to his douchebaggery.

"So what? I can get myself to my car."

The elevator dings open, and I step on, ready to push him off when he follows me.

Dammit.

"What do you say, princess?" he asks.

Is he serious?

"Are you kidding me? I would rather walk across broken glass the entire way than subject myself to a five-minute car ride with you. That's what I say."

Nostrils flaring, he reaches out and presses the emergency stop button without taking his eyes off me.

The elevator stops, the six-by-six space feeling smaller

with him in it. He crowds me against the wall, his body heat wrapping around me until I want to lean into him as much as I want to push him away.

"You have a snarky mouth."

"Pot, meet kettle," I tell him.

He angles impossibly closer. "Has anyone ever told you that?"

My mother. My sisters. My father. All of my teachers…

"So what?"

He responds with a quick dip as he claims my lips with his.

Oh, shit.

CHAPTER 5

EVAN

*F*uck.

   She tastes as good as she did last night.

No. Scratch that.

She tastes better.

It takes me a minute to place her signature flavor. Cupcakes. But there's more. A complexity, an undercurrent of rebellion. A spice not usually associated with my favorite birthday treat. And her lips against mine deliver on a promise made in sin.

I lean into her, cupping her jaw with both hands, and tilt her head into a position that allows me to drag my lips along the softly scented skin there.

"You drive me insane," I growl, nipping at the spot below her earlobe, holding her tighter when her knees buckle. Not like I'll let her fall.

My control snapping, I pin her hips with mine, my dick reaching for her heat, my hips pulsing against her.

"Evan." Her moan calls my attention back to her mouth, begging me to claim her lips once more and tangle my tongue with hers.

The call of my name on her lips is an aphrodisiac I can't deny, and I drag my hands down until my fingers flex against the flesh of her hips, digging in through the skintight leather pants that have driven me abso-fucking-lutely insane since she stepped out of her apartment building.

It took everything I had not to trace the smooth material up her long legs until I could find the silk of her skin. My dick has been hard since that initial thought and is now painfully digging into my zipper.

A sharp sting drags my attention back to the present and the woman digging her nails into the back of my neck, as lost in this moment as I am.

"Fuck." I break the kiss and trace hot, open-mouthed kisses down her neck and collarbone, then drop to where the swell of her breasts spills from her shirt.

"Did you wear this to get my attention?" I growl against her cleavage and explore with my tongue.

Her hips lift and press against mine, her ragged breathing obliterating all rational thought.

"Yes." She wraps one leg around my hip and pulls me closer.

I groan at the way the move makes her rub against my dick, even as I want to laugh at her audacity.

"Honest?" I ask and reward her admission with another swipe of my tongue while I grab both globes of her ass, lifting slightly and rubbing against the center seam of her pants.

"Mm-hmm." Leaving one hand in place, she pulls back and drops the other to cup me through the denim, and I swear to Christ my eyes roll back in my head at the pressure.

"Do you know how badly I want to fuck you right now? How I want to rip your pants down to your ankles and drive my cock deep inside your hot little pussy?"

Her whimper only fuels the fire.

"Do you want that too, princess?" I ask without lifting my mouth from the skin of her cleavage. Instead, I sink my teeth into the flesh under my lips when she doesn't respond right away. "Answer me."

She mewls and presses herself closer to my mouth. I accept her offering, sliding my lips over the exposed skin while I shift one hand to the snap of her pants and drag the zipper down until I encounter the smooth fabric of her panties.

I don't wait. I slide my hand beneath the cotton, too desperate to feel the softer skin beneath.

"*Evan.*"

My fingers slide through her folds to the bundle of nerves crying out for my attention.

"Your body is telling me, Lilah. But I want to hear the words on your lips. Tell me you fucking want me. That you want this." I slide one finger knuckle deep, keeping pressure on her clit with the pad of my thumb.

"Fuck. I want you."

Her eyes are squeezed shut. I don't fucking think so. She's going to admit it's me she wants. No one else.

"Who? Who do you want?"

Her eyes blaze open, the hazel a liquid gold as they meet mine.

"I want you to fuck me, Evan."

Hell yes.

I don't have the chance to respond before her lips capture mine, her tongue taking control until rational thought is all but gone.

The elevator's descent barely registers. I want to ignore the shift beneath my feet, focus on the pleasure at the tip of my fingers. Literally.

But I didn't start the elevator.

"Lilah."

"Mmm." She squeezes me tighter, and I nearly forget about our predicament.

"Princess."

I slowly pull back, cool air rushing into the space I put between us.

"The elevator."

Her eyes widen, and she brings shaky fingers to the fly of her pants.

Goddamn it.

She attempts another step back, but I snake out a hand and yank her to me.

"Where the fuck do you think you're going?"

"I—"

"We're not done with this conversation," I tell her and steal her lips in another kiss. This one tinged with the madness I'm giving into with every heartbeat.

"What conversation?" She licks her lips.

I'm about to dip my head for another taste when the elevator doors slide open and I'm locked in Chris's gaze. He darts a look at Lilah, then homes in on me again.

"What's going on in here?" His attention doesn't leave me. He just tilts his head and waits.

"Nothing." I shrug.

"Evan's giving me a ride to the mechanic," Lilah explains, her tone betraying a guilt I don't give a shit about.

We've done nothing to be ashamed of.

"Oh really?" Chris only raises an eyebrow.

"Ready?" I turn to Lilah, who looks more than eager to be done with this awkward conversation.

"Yeah. See you later, Chris." Lilah exits the elevator, and I follow, only to stop when Chris grabs my arm.

"Ev, you got a minute?" he asks.

Fuck.

"Yeah." I toss my keys to Lilah. "I'll be right there."

She walks away, and I meet Chris's gaze.

"What's up?"

"What's going on with you and Lilah?"

"Nothing."

"Nothing?" He cocks a brow again.

Damn, I want to tell my best friend exactly what's going on. But all I know is that I can't shake this unquenchable need for Lilah. Her taste. Her silken skin. All of her.

"You told me to be nice," I remind him.

"I did."

"I'm being nice."

"Uh-huh."

He doesn't buy any of the story I'm trying to sell.

"Anything else?" I ask.

"Just a reminder about the clause in our contract."

"Which one?" I ask. Like he isn't talking about the only one I've thought about endlessly over the last six goddamned months.

"The no-fraternization one."

Band members are forbidden from being involved with one another. Which wasn't a problem for the five of us guys who started Just One Yesterday in high school. It was never a question—until her.

Lilah.

"I remember."

He nods. "Okay."

"I'll see you later, man." I turn and walk toward the exit, sticking my hands in my pockets, only to be stopped by Chris once again.

"Hey, Ev?"

"Yeah?" I spin around one more time.

"That shade of lipstick really isn't your color." Chris smirks and punches the button, the elevator doors closing behind him as my hand shoots to my mouth.

Fuck.

That went well.

* * *

"How fucked am I?" I yell as I slam into Chris's house later that afternoon.

Normally, I might not use that as my greeting, but Gage is with his grandparents, so only Chris and Jessie are home.

Clue number one I know my brain is completely fucking gone?

I don't think about barging into the home of my best friend and his newly wedded wife.

"Shit. Sorry."

I spin around in the kitchen doorway, having gotten more of a visual than I wanted of said best friend between his wife's legs.

Jessie's squeak is followed by some rustling before Chris finally clears his throat.

"Knock much?"

Sighing, I turn around slowly, and Jessie is nowhere in sight.

"Sorry."

He waves me away. "I was half expecting you."

"Bullshit." My lips twitch, fighting a smile.

He flips me the bird but shrugs. "Can I help it if I got distracted?"

"Christopher!"

His shoulders hunch at the sound of Jessie's voice from the other room.

"Sorry, angel."

God, they're fucking adorable together.

"Obviously, you needed to talk," he says, turning his full attention back to me.

I nod. "About what you saw earlier…"

"What did I see earlier?" he asks.

"Dude," I say, "I know you know. You brought up the no-frat clause—"

He holds up a hand. "I don't give a fuck about that clause."

"You don't?"

"Cornerstone put it in there, and we ignored it because it didn't mean shit."

"Then why did you bring it up?"

"I need to make sure your head is somewhat engaged. The one on your shoulders," he clarifies with a smirk.

"Fuck you."

"You're not my type."

I groan and he laughs.

"Seriously," I tell him.

Chris's smile fades slightly. "Okay. Seriously. I'm fucking pissed at you. Why'd you lie?"

"Lie?"

"I thought you hated Lilah."

I shake my head. "I don't hate her."

"No shit, Sherlock. How long have you two been screwing around?"

"We're not."

He only raises an eyebrow.

"We're *not*. I kissed her. Twice."

I used to think hell was wanting Lilah as much as I did while watching her smile and joke with Milo. Now I know better. Hell isn't wanting Lilah. It's wanting her and having firsthand knowledge of what she tastes like, what she sounds like when her breath catches right before my lips claim hers. It's dropping her off at her car when all I want to do is take her home and claim her completely.

"What are you going to do now?"

"I should never have kissed her to begin with."

Or maybe I should still be kissing her.

Bad idea.

Probably.

Fuck, I don't know. How could a few kisses fuck with my head so badly?

"Is that what you want?"

"What does it matter what I want? Cornerstone already told us hands off."

"What about Lilah?"

"What about her?"

"God, you're a fucking idiot."

"Tell me something new," I snark back.

"Christ. What does she think about it?"

"How the fuck should I know?" I pace to the refrigerator and snag a bottle of water before slamming the door shut.

"Fucking ask. Don't wait. Do not pass go, do not collect two hundred dollars, do not do anything else until you fucking ask her what she wants."

Grabbing my arm, he drags me to the front door.

"Kicking me out already?"

"Damn straight. I have plans with my wife, and you have a question to go ask. Quit being a little bitch about it."

"Tell me how you really feel."

He smirks. "You never have to worry about that with me, Ev. You're like a brother to me, so I say this with love. Don't be a total fucking idiot."

"What about Cornerstone?"

"What about them?" he asks. "If you and Lilah belong together—if you two really do hide a shit-ton of lust under all the fucking bickering—we'll deal with Cornerstone."

He reaches out a hand, and I clasp his in mine before being yanked into a quick hug.

"Okay," I say, stepping back and shoving my hands in my pockets.

"And Ev?"

"Yeah?"

"Don't fucking hide shit from me. That's not who we are. We've never kept secrets."

"I…yeah, man, no more hiding shit."

Why did I? Fucking denial was making me delusional.

But I'm through denying myself of what I want.

No. Not what.

Who.

Lilah.

CHAPTER 6

LILAH

*H*ollie Berry I'm not.

While she's out claiming her coal and flipping a massive bird to the Adored Network, I've spent the last week avoiding Evan. A few dirty words and the brush of his fingers where I desperately craved them had me practically melting into an orgasmic puddle in the elevator.

Make no mistake about it, Evan Andrews is a world-class, grade-A, dirty talker. With extra credit. It was an unexpected but pleasant surprise.

If I was a woman bent on claiming her coal, the plan would have been to pick up where we left off as soon as the doors had closed on his car. But while I'm the black sheep of my family, I'm a quiet version. A silent rebel. I need time to sort out how I feel about Evan's growled words against my skin and how his fingers played my goddamn body like a fiddle.

Did I like it? Hell fucking yes.

Did it confuse the shit out of me? Also yes.

So I've been avoiding him as much as possible, showing up at the last minute for rehearsals and our sound check and then ducking out as soon as we finish. Because I need my wits about me and my armor in place when he's around, and I don't want to take a chance on being alone with him. Only now it's the night of the concert and there's no sign of him. Maybe because I showed up crazy early for this event. I even showed up before Chris, and he's usually the first to arrive to everything.

I'm sitting in a chair in our dressing room when the door creaks open. I spin, but the words die on my lips when Finn walks through the door.

"Hey, Lil." He waves halfheartedly before collapsing onto the couch along the wall.

"Hey." I chew on my lower lip, cursing when I catch a peek of myself in the mirror and realize I need to reapply the red stain to my lips.

Later.

"What's up?"

"Hmm?" I ask distractedly.

"What's up? I don't think I've ever seen you look this antsy before."

I stop my knee from bouncing like a jackhammer against the chair and curl my fingers around it.

"Nothing," I manage to squeak out.

Finn only cocks an eyebrow and continues to stare at me with his unreadable gaze until I sigh.

"Where's Evan?" I ask. My voice is a far cry from the nonchalance I wish was there, breaking over Evan's name like a sixteen-year-old fangirl.

"Ev?"

I don't blame him for his confusion. Usually, Evan and I repel each other like magnets.

"Not sure. Maybe Chris knows," he continues.

"Maybe Chris knows what?" Chris steps through the door mid-conversation, with Jessie's hand gripped firmly in his.

"Lilah was asking about Evan," Finn explains.

"You know Evan." He shrugs.

Chris's response is so cryptic it makes me want to scream. No, no, I don't. Or maybe I thought I did. Maybe I thought that kiss meant I understood him more than I actually do.

"My bigger question is where the fuck is Milo," Chris huffs, focusing his attention on Finn since the two of them are always together.

"He said he had shit to do and would see me later," Finn explains.

"What could he possibly have to do?" Chris asks.

As if speaking his name conjures him, Milo steps through the door, though he's nearly unrecognizable. Gone is the ever-present man bun and the cocky grin, replaced by a short-haired version of our carefree drummer.

He folds in on himself under the intensity of our combined scrutiny. With a quick shake of his head, he steps farther into the room.

"What the fuck are you all staring at?"

Neither Finn nor Chris says anything, so I finally speak up.

"What happened to your hair?"

He laughs and runs a hand through what's left of his hair —which isn't much, given the close crop—but the movement is awkward, self-conscious.

"I cut it."

"I can see that. Why?"

Milo's worn his hair long since Just One Yesterday took off. His shoulder-length light-brown locks have always been synonymous with the drummer.

He shrugs and barely manages to meet my eyes before his gaze skitters again.

"It was...time for a change."

He's not giving us the full story. I open my mouth to ask him, but he keeps talking.

"Anyone check on Ev lately?"

"Evan? He's here?" I ask.

"Bathroom."

Milo's one-word response is followed immediately by a groan from Chris.

"I thought he was over that."

"Over what?" I ask.

Is he sick?

Finn snorts a laugh. "It's gotten better. But no way will it ever go away."

"What won't go away?"

"Do you remember our first tour?" Milo asks, and both Chris and Finn chuckle.

"What the hell is going on?" Tired of being ignored, I raise my voice to grab their attention.

Chris looks at me for the first time. His eyes flash with the sudden recognition. *Finally*, he remembers that I have no idea what they're talking about. How could I when I joined the band six months ago?

"Evan's anxiety skyrockets before every show. He has an almost crippling fear of performing or speaking in public." His explanation is matter-of-fact. Practically rehearsed.

"What?" I've never heard about it. Not in any article about them I've read over the years.

Chris nods. "During our first tour, Evan threw up before every show. It was so bad that he wouldn't eat at all the day of a show."

"But he's our lead singer."

"He is. But haven't you ever wondered why I'm JOY's spokesperson and not him? Why he doesn't say much when he's not on stage?"

I hadn't given it much thought.

"I assumed with your parents' background, it made more sense for you to take on that role," I say.

He nods. "It played into it, but it wasn't the driving factor." He studies me for several moments, his brown eyes thoughtful, before he steps closer and speaks again. "Will you check on him?"

"Me?" I ask.

"He needs you." The words are murmured, meant only for my ears, but based on the encouraging smile Jessie sends my way, she overheard.

He needs me.

Three small words, but they hold the power to drive me from the room with no other thought than to check on Evan. I find him leaning against the wall, head down, in the bathroom backstage. My heels tap against the tile in a slight staccato rhythm as I move closer. He tips his face up when I drop to my haunches in front of him. Dark circles mar the skin surrounding his eyes. He's pale, almost green, and covered in a light sheen of perspiration, but I can't think of a time when I've been as attracted to him as I am in this moment.

The one where he moves from fantasy to reality.

"Hey," I say, my voice quiet in the echoing bathroom.

"Hi," he croaks out.

Gone are all my thoughts about avoiding him, about what to say about our kiss in the elevator. All I want is to help him. I don't stop myself from lifting a hand to cup his jaw, from loving the way he leans into my touch. I simply soak in the moment.

"You okay?"

Stupid question given the pallor of his skin and the deep purple smudges under his eyes. But my brain is recalibrating.

"I'll be fine. The guys told you?"

I nod. "Yeah. I didn't know."

My thighs are starting to protest the extended time on the

balls of my feet, but I attempt to ignore their protests. I breathe a sigh of relief when Evan shifts to stand and tugs me up with him.

"It's not something I talk about."

"I figured."

Does he realize his hands are on my hips? Or am I the only one hyperaware of the connection that exists between us?

"I've been this way for as long as I can remember. Since those little performances in elementary school—do you remember those?" he asks but doesn't wait for my response. "Maybe you didn't do them."

"I didn't," I admit. "But I had recitals."

Recitals where nearly every student had someone in the audience to cheer them on. The only time that happened for me was when Aunt Sarah was in town.

"Were you ever nervous?"

I shake my head. "I can remember wanting to do well, but more to prove my worth to my parents so maybe they would come to one of my recitals, but I don't think it was nerves."

It was the desire to be loved. To gain their attention.

"Princess."

He tugs on my hips until I'm pressed against him, his lips searing against my forehead in a kiss that overwhelms my whole body. Maybe this sweetness should confuse me after the heat of the kiss in the elevator. But it doesn't. It gives me insight into who he is. He's intensity and he's tenderness. And I'm in danger of falling head over heels for this man instead of only lusting after him.

Stepping back, I clear my throat, but he doesn't let me get too far, refusing to loosen the hold he has on me.

"Enough about me. What about you?" I ask.

"What about me?"

"How do you get ready for shows? What can I do to help?"

His hands flex against the leather covering my hips. Given the distracted look on his face, the motion was likely involuntary. But the way his thumbs immediately rub against my hip bones contradicts that notion.

"It usually goes away on its own."

"When?" I bite my lip to hold back a moan when he realigns our lower bodies and presses his erection against my stomach.

"The end of the first song." His voice drops to a murmur while he zeros in on my mouth.

"So you just—what—are like this until then? Nothing helps?" My question is breathy, my lips tingling under his scrutiny and my lungs laboring to breathe normally.

There is no normal. Not with him.

So why am I fighting against this? And how did we go from concern and empathy to this fire so quickly? Regardless of how, I'm tired of thinking about it. It's time to *do* something.

Time to claim your coal, Lilah.

I drag my hands up his arms and loop them around his neck, pulling him down until we're breathing each other in.

"There's something I haven't tried. Maybe you could help me," he says.

"What's that?"

"Maybe all I need is a good distraction."

"So anything will do?"

"No, princess. Only you."

His lips fasten to mine on the last word, his tongue seeking entrance, running along mine when I let him in. I moan, the sound captured in the fusion of our lips but loud enough to encourage him to grip the fabric covering my hips.

With both hands, he boosts me, and I wind my legs

around his hips while he settles me on the sink. His erection presses against the seam of my pants, tempting me to rage against the fabric still separating us. Breaking the kiss, he drags hot, open-mouthed kisses back to my ear, his teeth tugging at the sensitive skin of my neck. I find the back of his head with my fingers and run my nails lightly along the hairline until a trail of goose bumps ripples across his skin.

"Fuck." He moans and rubs against the light contact, encouraging me to repeat the motion.

"Do you like that?"

His response is another tease of his lips while he cups my breast through the thin Just One Yesterday T-shirt I'm wearing. Since I'm not wearing a bra, his thumb drags along the nipple, and I bend backward to give him more access to the area, luxuriating in the repetition of his caress.

"Do you like what I'm doing to you?" The timbre of his deep voice resonates in my core and creates a pulsing response.

"*Yes.*"

"I want you. Right here, right now."

"Yes," I moan again. "Now. Here."

"There's no escaping this time."

Escape? Who's thinking about escape?

"Ev? You in there? Five minutes." Chris pounds once on the door.

Evan and I break apart like guilty teenagers once again.

"We'll pick this back up later," I say, sliding off the counter, unsurprised when he doesn't back up or give me space.

"We will definitely pick this back up later," he says. "The only question is your room or mine?"

CHAPTER 7

EVAN

*I*f someone were to ask me about our first show since Noah's departure, I'd probably stumble all over the lack of details I retained. The set blurs into a mass of cheers from the crowd, the elation that hits every time we play our music, and the way Lilah's voice blends with mine.

Lilah.

Fuck.

After talking to Chris, I spent the week trying to work up the nerve to call her. But what if it was only the heat of the moment sparking for her when the heat simmered inside me constantly?

I got my answer tonight though. Leaning against the bathroom wall, I willed myself not to puke. Then she was rushing in and dropping in front of me like a gift from heaven made for sin. Sky-high red heels, black leather pants molding to every mouth-watering curve, and a band T-shirt tied with a mass of knots at the back rather than the fabric that used to be there.

But it was the way she cupped my face that did it for me, the genuine concern so clear in her big hazel eyes. She doesn't hate me any more than I hate her. And now that our encore is over, I have plans. Ones involving my hotel room and both of us naked.

The crowd is still cheering beyond the closed curtain when I spin from the mic and meet her at the side of her setup. I don't give her a chance to say anything. I just pick up the kiss right where we left off, not giving a fuck that we're in full view of the guys and anyone else wandering backstage.

Gliding my tongue along the seam of her lips, I wait for her to let me in, fusing my mouth to hers when she finally opens on a gasp. Her fingers are clenched in the fabric of my shirt, and the little whimper that escapes when I yank her against me adds more fuel to the fire. By the time I finally gentle the kiss to break it, we're the only two band members on stage, surrounded only by the crew tearing down the equipment around us.

"Wow." Her word is a breath of air against the fingers she lifts to the swollen flesh of her lips.

My dick punches against my zipper, and I grit my teeth at the need to pull her in for more.

"I want you."

Three words. They're simple, but I don't have the brain-power to make them prettier for her, to give her the sentiments she deserves. But her response brings me to my knees.

"You have me."

I don't waste any time. We're stumbling down the hall toward my hotel room less than ten minutes later. Pressing her back against the door once we're inside, I lift her until she wraps her legs around my waist and the heels of her shoes prick into my lower back, pulling me tighter against her.

Head dipped forward, I nip at her lower lip before soothing the sting with my tongue.

"Are you sure?"

Thoughts of the silent car ride here have me second-guessing. I need to know we're still on the same page.

Her response is to tunnel her fingers into my hair and yank my mouth to hers.

"Yes," she says, her lips brushing mine. "I'm sure."

Tightening those gorgeous fucking legs around my waist again, she pulls me impossibly closer.

I groan and drop my head to sink my teeth into her shoulder. "Hold on." I rush the fifteen steps from the door to the bed and lower her, thankful I left the light on so I can witness her every reaction. One heel drops to the floor followed by the other, and her hands shift to the button on her pants.

"No," I tell her.

"No?"

I drop to the mattress next to her and knock her fingers out of the way.

"I'll take care of those." I can't resist running my hand along her thigh and between them when she parts her legs. The leather barrier is as much of a turn-on as it is a hindrance, as is the way she lifts her hips to follow my palm as it glides up.

Her mouth beckons to me again, and I settle between her thighs, dragging my lips back and forth across hers until she plants her palms on either side of my face, stopping me from moving away.

"Kiss me."

Smiling against her lips, I give her what she demands, reacquainting myself with her unique flavor. Fuck. How does she always taste like cupcakes?

"How?" I ask, pulling away to trail my lips down her throat.

"How what?" Her voice is husky, her hands roaming my back as I continue my path down her body.

"You taste like cupcakes."

Her eyes pop open, hazed over. "What?"

"Cupcakes."

"I—my lip gloss? It's sugar cookie flavored."

I shake my head to negate that argument.

"It's you. You taste so fucking good." With a groan, I nip at her collarbone, partially hidden under the fabric of her altered concert tee.

She mewls, running her nails down my back until she can cup my ass. Given the layers of clothing between us, I can only imagine the heat of her pussy against me, but I don't fucking care. My imagination is plenty. For now.

I drop my mouth to one of the puckered nipples straining against the thin cotton material and suck, tonguing the fabric around the point until she writhes against me. Only then do I sink my teeth into her slowly and tug.

"*Evan.*"

"You like that, princess?"

I repeat the caress, finding the waistband of her pants at the same time and following the smooth skin to the button I flick open with ease.

"Yes. *Yes.*" Her original whisper turns to a whimper at the second sting.

"I want to rip this shirt off you. To worship your breasts until you're coming undone and begging me for more."

Her legs shudder around my waist, and her ragged breathing grows shallower. Delving my hands beneath her, I shift us until we're both leaning up and I can toy with the strings left at the back of her shirt. Flexing slightly, I pull until one string breaks, followed by another.

"Ev."

"Stop me." Another string, and her shirt gapes in the front.

She shakes her head, and with a shout, I rip every remaining knot apart until I can toss the ruined top to the side of the bed. The tips of her breasts are beaded, and my mouth waters for a taste without the fabric barrier. I lay her back down again, barely hanging on to the vestiges of control I have left.

Releasing her, I trail a path down her arm with my fingertips—gooseflesh rises, the rosy tips of her breasts tightening more. Tanned skin disappears into the leather still clinging to her hips, but I'm drawn back to her quivering breasts, captivated by the way they beg for my touch. For my kiss. Her hands shift restlessly at her sides, like she doesn't know what to do with them, so I grab one and rest it against my aching cock.

"This is what you do to me." I squeeze, reinforcing her hold on me. "Every time I kiss you. Every time I think about getting my hands on you."

She curls her fingers, and my dick kicks against her palm. When her tongue darts out to moisten her lips, all rational thought is driven out by the surge of lust that takes over. My lips find one of those tight buds, and I lean over, forcing her flat and giving me better access to the nipple not currently the center of attention of my mouth.

The combination of nipping one breast with my teeth and pinching the opposite one makes her squirm against the bed as she seeks friction in her slick pants.

"I bet you're fucking soaked right now, aren't you, princess? You like when my teeth mark your body." I nip at the swell of one breast to emphasize my point, and her hands fist the cotton of my shirt. "Can I make you come with my mouth alone?" I suck on her nipple again before I release her with a pop. "Or with my fingers?"

I pluck the other peak between my forefinger and thumb until she whimpers.

"Or both?"

Switching sides, I drag my tongue around the distended point, red from my ministrations, while I palm the breast still wet from my mouth.

"*Evan.*"

"I'm going to make you come like this, princess." I growl the promise against her sweat-slicked skin and focus on moving back and forth between her breasts, alternating my mouth and hands, my pace, everything I can, until her arms strain to hold me to her.

"Please." Her plea is music to my ears, but I'm not stopping until I make her come this way.

My dick is screaming to join in the action, to sink into her heat, but I ignore it to shift to her other breast again and tug at the ruby-red tip with my teeth.

"On your knees, baby." I roll her until she lifts to all fours under me and pulse my hips against her ass. Starting at one shoulder, I kiss my way across and nuzzle her hair away from her neck while I find her breasts again and cup the warm weight.

At the first tug of my fingers, her hips practically collapse, so I slide one of my legs between hers to keep her upright.

"You're fucking close, aren't you, princess? Ready for me to make you explode? Make you scream my name?"

She nods her head furiously and drives her hips back against me, grinding against my dick, eliciting the most incredible pain.

"Tell me."

"I want to come. Please make me come."

"Like this? With my fingers tugging at your breasts and my teeth sinking into your shoulder?"

I nip at the tendon where her neck and shoulder meet.

"Yes!"

"That won't be it. I'm going to make you come on my tongue and with my fingers before I finally fill up that pretty pussy of yours. I bet it's begging for me right now, huh?" I cup her through the leather, and she presses into my palm before I take my hand away and move it back to her breast. "Not quite there, princess. What about coming for me right now?"

I use both thumbs and index fingers to apply steady pressure on each of her nipples as I twist slightly, pulling an audible gasp from her.

"If you want my face between your legs, you need to come right the fuck now. Do you hear me? Right now." I growl and sink my teeth roughly into her shoulder and simultaneously twist her nipples.

She wails, and her hips rock back and forth erratically as her orgasm overtakes her.

"Fuck, that's it, baby. Just like that."

She collapses, trapping my hands under her breasts, and she moans at the friction. I shift until my hands are free and run them down her back until I reach the waist of her pants, but I pause with my hands resting there.

"More?" I ask.

She nods. "Don't stop."

I pull the waistband of her pants down, exposing the strip of red lace between the cheeks of her ass. Damn. My dick pulses in my jeans at the hot as fuck vision.

"Why would I stop? I promised you more orgasms."

She moans, and I slide my finger behind the string and run it back and forth across the lace. The smell of her arousal infuses the air.

"I'm not finished with you yet, princess."

I doubt I ever will be. With another tug, her panties are

shredded lace in my hand. Only then do I work her pants all the way down her legs.

She's a fucking goddess stretched across the dark blue of the bedspread, skin glowing in the dim light. I shed my own pants and shirt before lying back on the bed while my dick points to the ceiling. Reaching over my head, I lift her and slide under her until her pussy is right where I want it.

Fuck.

"You smell so fucking good, princess." I breathe deep. "So...fucking...good." With my tongue, I trace her slit from back to front.

"*Evan.*" My name is a long moan, muffled where she's got her face buried in the sheets, making my dick leak at the sound.

"Mmm." I bury my tongue in her pussy. Vanilla, sugar, and spice. "You're mine now."

And I'll be damned if I'm giving her up after this.

CHAPTER 8

LILAH

J'm dragged from a deep sleep by warm lips caressing my shoulder.

"Good morning." The words are a delicious growl. One I know I'll never get out of my head.

Not after last night.

Not that I'd want to.

Rolling over, I wince at the soreness in neglected muscles.

Evan's watching me, searching my expression. "Are you okay?"

My smile is soft, trembling around the edges. This man doesn't have a hateful bone in his body. Why didn't I see that until now?

"I'm fine. Just a little sore." I huff a laugh.

He can't quite hide the smirk tilting his lips, but the kiss he presses to my mouth is gentle, and instead of taking it further, he drops down to the bed and pulls me into the crook of his arm.

"I should have been more gentle."

I sit up and watch him, waiting until he meets my gaze to speak.

"Last night was perfect. I just…I haven't…for a while."

"For me too."

Taking in his toned chest and arms, I seriously doubt that.

"You look skeptical."

"I am. I mean, look at you. You're Evan Freaking Andrews, lead singer of Just One Yesterday."

"So?"

"So, I'm sure there are plenty of women—"

"Groupies."

I roll my eyes. "Fine. There are probably hundreds of groupies who would kill to be with you. They'd jump at the chance."

"I don't want groupies."

His cobalt-blue eyes are serious when I hazard a glance at him.

"You don't?"

"I haven't wanted anyone else in months, princess. Six, to be exact."

"Six?"

How long since I joined the band? Half a year?

He nods. "Since the moment you walked into the studio space for your audition, you've been the only one to capture my attention."

"But you hated me."

"I didn't. But I knew I couldn't be with you."

"Why not?"

"The no-fraternization clause Cornerstone included in all our contracts. Band members aren't allowed to date one another. It was never a problem when it was Noah playing keyboards. No offense to him, but I've seen his naked ass more times than I care to count."

He smiles at my giggle.

"Now, your ass…" He lifts me to straddle him, his hands

squeezing the sides of my ass to rub me against his hardening cock.

Moaning, I lean my head back, relishing the way the friction incites an inferno just below my sensitive flesh. When he stops, I open my eyes to find him staring up at me.

"What?" I ask, trying to ignore the self-conscious creep of doubt along the edges.

"I know why I'm here. I couldn't resist you anymore. But what about you? I thought you hated me too. Although your sneer is more adorable than intimidating."

I try to look angry but fail, given the way his grin only grows at my feigned frustration.

Finally, I drop my arms, and his hands find mine to weave our fingers together.

"I—I'm attracted to you too. Even when you were an asshole to me," I say.

He squeezes my fingers in apology, his expression full of regret.

"You tease me about being someone I'm not. I'll never be a good trophy wife like my mom and my sisters. But I'm not a full-on rebel either. I'm tired of not being happy, so I'm doing what Hollie Berry did. I'm claiming my coal for Christmas."

"Hollie Berry?" he asks.

I explain what's going on and how she's figuring out what she wants for herself. Like me.

"Claiming your coal, huh?" He sits up suddenly so we're nose to nose. His lips brush against mine twice in teasing caresses before he pulls back. "What do you say we really land on Santa's naughty list, then?"

I'm on my back before I can say anything, his tongue plundering my mouth until he's once more cradled between my thighs and I can wrap my legs around his waist.

"Fuck," he groans, breaking the kiss. "Aren't you sore?"

I lift my hips, his hard dick sliding through my folds and turning me on more.

"Not sore enough to stop this."

"Goddamn, princess, the heat of your pussy calls to me like a siren. Like a fucking drug I can't deny." He pushes forward, the head of his dick lining up with my entrance, and I shiver as delight tingles up my spine.

But he shifts again and drags his lips down my neck, nipping at the tendon where it meets my shoulder before soothing the sting with his tongue.

"Evan." His name is a broken moan.

He moves his mouth lower, across my collarbone to the swell of my breasts.

"Let me," he says.

Whatever he wants, he can have.

I'm his.

Fingers spread wide, I tunnel through his hair, gripping the strands and dragging his mouth to my nipple. He chuckles before swirling his tongue around the stiff peak.

"God, you taste like fucking heaven." He continues his assault on my breasts, licking me like a goddamned lollipop before tugging me into his mouth to nibble at the beaded tip. His hand comes up to play with my other breast, echoing the movements that made me come the first time last night.

My breasts have never been this sensitive. Probably because no one has ever paid such reverent attention to them.

Not like Evan.

"Have I told you how much I love your breasts?" He switches sides before releasing me fully.

I mewl in disappointment as cool air washes over the puckered tip.

"I'd worship your breasts all day if I could, but I want to end my pilgrimage in a sweeter place."

His hair tickles the skin of my abdomen, making me shift my thighs restlessly against his chest. He shoulders them apart, pushing my thighs back and exposing me to him. The warm breath of his words caresses my skin as he closes the distance, but he pauses before he puts his mouth where I need him most.

"*Please.*" My thighs tighten around his shoulders, and I lift my hips, hoping to direct him to where I want him.

"Please, what?" he asks and shifts infinitely closer. He purses his lips and blows gently on my pussy. "Please, this?"

He cups my breast, his fingers working the nipple. My hips jump, bringing me into contact with his chin.

"*Evan.*"

"Please, this?" His voice grows thicker by the moment, and he drags his tongue from the back to the front, swirling around my clit.

I fist the sheets on the outside of my thighs, gripping the fabric tight, my orgasm already barreling toward me like a freight train.

He stops long enough to unfurl the abused cloth from my fingers, lifting each hand to his head. Only when both of my hands tangle in his hair does he continue his oral exploration. Long strokes are alternated with pulsing taps.

"You taste so fucking good," he growls against me before diving back in.

My only response is to chant his name between broken breaths.

"I need you to come, princess," he says as he slides one finger knuckle deep, then adds a second, stretching me slightly. My walls flutter around the digits until he curls them and sucks my clit into his mouth. The slight pressure on my G-spot combined with the strong suction is all it takes for me to explode, my orgasm cresting and burying me in white lights of pleasure, my body riding the wave while simultaneously riding his fingers. I hold him against me with my hands in his hair, and my thighs squeezed tight to his ears while he licks and sucks until the pleasure is too much and I squirm away.

"I-I-I can't. No more."

I remind myself to uncurl my fingers from his hair, and he chuckles, the vibrations and the last lick he gives me making me gasp.

"No?"

"No. I want you." I pull slightly at his hair until he crawls back up my body.

"You have me," he says, claiming my lips again.

I moan at the taste of myself on his lips while my legs wrap around his waist.

"Inside me," I pant, pressing my heels against his ass to push him where I want him.

"Princess. I need a condom." His voice is gritty, like he's fighting for control, and I fucking love it.

"I'm on birth control," I admit, lifting my hips and holding myself against his dick by pulling my legs tighter around him.

"Fuck. Are you sure?" he asks. He's not asking if I'm sure about my form of contraception.

Am I sure about this next step?

"Yes. I want you." My lips find his jaw, and I'm overcome by the need to sink my teeth into his skin. "Now."

He doesn't waste any time lining up his dick at my entrance and filling me with one thrust.

"Fuck. Yes." The muscles in his neck strain as another orgasm builds.

He rolls us until he's propped against the pillows, and I grind against him, my breasts bouncing as my head falls back on a moan.

"That's it, baby. Ride my cock."

The orgasm shimmers at the edges, my pussy tightening around his dick until he's moaning with me.

"I-I-I'm going to come."

"I can feel you. Come for me. Right now. Right fucking now," he demands.

Lightning strikes of pleasure arc from where he pulses inside me and travel out into the rest of my body. By the time I come back to reality, I'm boneless against his chest, his hands drawing small patterns on my back while the beat of his heart races against my cheek.

"I should get up."

He tightens his arms around me. "Why?"

"I need to shower. Get a change of clothes."

"Don't go."

"You want to stay like this until we leave?"

He pulses his hips, and I whimper at the aftershocks his movement creates.

"What's wrong with that? Knowing that I'm dripping down this sweet pussy? You bet your ass I want that."

My core spasms at his words.

He moans at the sensation. "See? Perfect."

"I'm far from perfect."

"Princess, you're pretty fucking perfect for me, and that's what counts."

Fucking swoon.

"What are we going to tell everyone?" I ask, unsure where this next step takes us.

I like him. I think he likes me.

But there's the no-fraternization clause.

"What's there to tell?"

I lift my head from his chest to meet his eyes.

"What's there to tell?" I repeat.

"Everyone saw me kiss you last night like you were the oxygen mask on a crashing airplane."

I snort a laugh. "That's a great analogy. A plane crash."

"I'm not good at all the flowery word bullshit. There's a reason why Chris writes the songs. He and Noah..."

He grows quiet at the mention of JOY's original keyboardist. The way he always does. The way all the guys do. I'm not going to lie. It still stings when that happens. Like I'm not enough.

But most of me understands. They're worried for their friend, for their brother who is battling demons none of them could help him face.

"You're pretty good at saying things I like to hear," I assure him. "But even better at dirty talk."

His laughter bursts out of him as he presses his lips against my neck.

"You like that, huh?"

I gasp as his length hardens once more and his whiskers tickle my neck.

"I do. Want to tell me some more?"

"You bet your ass I do."

CHAPTER 9

EVAN

"*I*'m about sick of you fucking guys not listening to a goddamn word I say," Marcus rants.

He's been at it for over an hour, and his shade has shifted from beet red to mottled and splotchy, but his skin tone hasn't been close to a natural hue since we got here.

I spare a glance at Chris, who meets my gaze with a roll of his eyes. He's as nonplussed by Marcus's latest monologue as I am. Unfortunately, I happen to be the subject, so I'm somewhat obligated to tune in here and there to what this pompous asshat with a comb-over is ranting about.

"We have a no-fraternization clause"—he pokes a finger at the flagged section in front of me—"for a reason."

"We originally requested to strike that out," Chris says from his side of the table.

Marcus glances up at him. "And we agreed it would remain when we altered the creative clause that allows you five to retain your music rights unless you choose to cede control over a song."

"And that's how Cornerstone got 'Imagine My Touch,'" Chris fires back.

God, that song was incredible. One of Noah's best. But it wasn't one we could use, so we sold the rights to Cornerstone.

"If I remember correctly, that was a number one single for the artist who recorded it," I can't help but chime in.

A vein in Marcus's forehead pulses in response, and he claps a hand over it.

"Why am I reading reports about you kissing Lilah after the concert in San Francisco?"

News about our kiss made it back to LA in record time. Not sure how since our roadies have always been loyal to us, but Chris and I were investigating on our own. And there was no need for Lilah, Finn, or Milo to be at today's meeting. Finn and Milo are doing whatever Finn and Milo do when not under adult supervision, and Lilah is waiting for me at her apartment. The plan is to watch some Hollie Berry Christmas movies she bought. Meanwhile, I want to spend as much fucking time with her as possible.

She's funny and cute and so damn sexy that I spend most of my time around her hard for her and the rest of the time buried inside her.

In other words, I'm in big trouble.

"I did kiss Lilah after the concert." I won't lie about it. I have no reason to hide it since we've done nothing wrong.

"And what about the clause?"

"Fuck the clause."

Chris's lips twitch at my response, and I struggle to bite back my own smile.

"It's part of your contract."

"I don't give a shit what the contract says. That clause has been in there for years when it didn't need to be. Lilah and I are two consenting adults, and what we do in our personal lives is none of the label's fucking business. What we're doing isn't illegal, nor will our actions jeopardize your fucking reputation." That said, I push back from the table. "Now, if you're through with this broken record routine, I'm leaving. I have better shit to do with my time than listen to you scream."

I step out of the room as Marcus blusters a response, relieved when the closing door cuts off the next asinine thing to spew from his mouth. At the elevator bank, I lean against the wall and wait. Chris isn't far behind me, and when he steps from the room, I push the button that will call the elevator.

We're silent as we wait, conscious of the receptionist in the lobby, who studies us like she's actually an undercover paparazzo. Maybe she is. I wouldn't put it past these vultures. But we don't give her anything to talk about, waiting instead until we're in the elevator.

"That was bullshit," I say.

Chris nods. "It was. I figured it wouldn't be easy, but it's also not like this is a huge deal. They have other artists with bigger problems."

"Did Marcus say anything after I left?"

"Nah. I think he'd said all he had to say, and when we didn't immediately apologize and kiss his ass, he wasn't sure what to do with us."

"Fuck. What are we going to do about this?"

"If you're as serious about Lilah as I figure you are, there are a few options. This is not the first time severing ties with Cornerstone has crossed my mind. Especially after all the bullshit they pulled with Noah."

"So leave? And go where? Arrhythmic?" Arrhythmic is the name of the label Chris's brother-in-law, Jax Bryant, co-owns with Nick Rhodes. I snort. "Yeah, Cornerstone wouldn't lose their shit too much if we dropped them for the same label they lost Dylan Graves to."

Chris shrugs. "Cornerstone has changed, Ev. Now all they

want is mass-market shit. I'm not into that. Neither are you or Finn or Milo."

"Or Lilah."

He smirks. "Glad to see you finally saying her name while *not* wearing a scowl."

"Asshole." I flip him the bird as we exit the elevator. "We're actually doing this?"

It's strange to consider leaving the label that gave us our shot so many years ago. But we've all changed. Just One Yesterday is no longer the five guys from high school who took their shot and miraculously succeeded. Noah is in an intense rehab program that will hopefully be successful this time. Chris is married and has a kid. Even Milo and Finn don't pull the same stupid shit they used to. Lilah and I are... doing whatever it is we're doing. We haven't slept apart since the night of the concert last weekend.

Maybe it's time for a change.

I head straight to Lilah's after Cornerstone, thankful her apartment is so close. Most people are too busy with holiday shopping or whatever to notice me walking down the block with no security in sight.

I knock on the door and open it when Lilah calls to come in, ready to ream her ass about leaving the fucking door unlocked. Yes, her building has security, but that doesn't make it foolproof. But the words die on my lips when I find her lying on the floor by the Christmas tree, attention fixed on me.

Holy. Fucking. Shit.

"Princess."

All the blood rushes from my brain to my dick, making speech impossible in the wake of the image before me. Her blond hair is curled and pulled back into a ponytail, and her red lips match the color of the sexy Santa suit that hugs her body in red silk and soft fur.

"Care to have Santa sit on *your* lap?" she asks, lifting onto her knees provocatively and bending first one leg and the other to rise from the ground.

I collapse into the chair she motions to.

"What do you have planned, Mrs. Claus?"

"It depends," she says with a sly grin. "Have you been a good boy or a naughty one?"

I cup her hips and yank her to me.

"Naughty. Definitely. How many times have we claimed your coal?"

She slaps my hands with hers and pushes them both to the arms of the chair.

"Naughty boys don't get to touch."

"We'll see about that," I grumble.

Her teeth sink into her lower lip, but I can see the way she struggles to contain her smile. She presses a button on her phone, and the intro to "Santa Baby" kicks through a speaker somewhere in her living room. She leans over, her tongue rimming my ear before she nibbles the lobe.

"Sit still and wait here. If you're good, Santa may bring you a present."

My fingers curl into the fabric of the chair, and my dick is already digging into the zipper of my jeans, but I nod, curious about what type of present she has in mind.

She steps back, taking the smell of vanilla and sugar with her, but only far enough to dance. A dance meant only for me. She grinds and gyrates, finally unveiling her perfect fucking body hidden under the little negligee. On the front of her panties is a little bow with a tag.

"Is that for me?" I barely recognize the sound of my voice beneath the grit.

"Yes," she says, and I start to rise, only to be pushed back down again with a hand to the chest. "Not yet."

Her hands trail along my arms as she steps between my parted thighs, running along my shirt until she reaches the fly of my jeans and flicks the button open. The immediate pressure relief is palpable but still not quite what I need.

"Lilah."

She sinks down to her knees and palms my length through the denim before her fingers slide the zipper down carefully, letting my dick spring free.

"Hmm. Is this for Santa?" she asks, wrapping her fingers around my length and tugging slightly.

"Fuck."

"Such a bad word from a boy who promised to be good."

"Keep playing, princess. I'll show you exactly how bad I can be when I impale you with my cock."

She squeezes harder, just as turned on by this as I am.

"You want that, baby? You want to ride my cock for Christmas?"

Her breath breaks, and she shakes her head to clear the spell my words cast over her.

"Not yet. First, I want to..." Her voice trails off as she lowers to the floor in front of me.

It isn't until her lips wrap around the end of my cock that her words hit me. Over the last few days, we've experienced fast sex and slow sex. This is one of those times where she wants to go fast—after her teasing. She lowers onto my cock until I bump the back of her throat, and she swallows around me while tracing the vein on the underside of my shaft with her tongue.

Pulsing my hips, I moan while my fingers scrabble for purchase on the smooth chair. Her throat convulses around me, and I struggle to remember my own goddamned name, but the hair tickling my arms reminds me of her ponytail, and I wrap it around one of my hands while she continues to bob on my cock.

"That's it, baby. Wrap those pretty red lips around me and take me. Fuck, princess, your mouth feels so goddamn good right now."

She hums, the vibration settling in the base of my spine as my orgasm continues to build.

"How long did you plan this? Today?"

She hums again, and I lift my hips, driving my cock a little deeper down her throat.

"Goddamn, I'm so close, princess. Really fucking close to coming in that sweet little mouth of yours. Do you want that?"

Her suction intensifies, and stars dance behind my eyes.

"Fuck, yes, you do. Should I do it? Should I fuck that sassy mouth of yours before I slide my dick into your pussy?"

She nods, so I increase my tempo until my vision tunnels. My only reality is the woman practically in my lap. Her breasts bounce with every thrust of my hips, and her mouth feels fucking incredible wrapped around my dick. But this isn't what I want.

The fuck it isn't.

I want more than a quick blow job. Right now, I want to drive my dick into her pussy and claim her skin with my lips. I manage to pop her off my dick and lift her into my arms as I stand and lay us both down in the glow of her illuminated Christmas tree.

"Why'd you stop?" She studies me, her brow furrowed and that damn lip caught between her teeth.

I claim her mouth, pouring every emotion I've suppressed over the last six months into the kiss. This isn't simply lust for me. It's so much fucking more. And I need her to realize I'm all in. For her. For us.

She moans and wraps her legs around my waist,

reminding me that my jeans are barely hanging on. Standing, I whip off my T-shirt and kick off my jeans and boxers until I'm naked in front of her. She gives me a once-over, her tongue slicking along her lips. Kneeling again, I reach for her panties and tug them down her legs.

"You wrapped your pussy up so pretty, princess. Call me a naughty boy, but I never could wait until Christmas to see what I was getting."

She parts her legs so I can glide my fingers through her folds and find the bundle of nerves swollen with need and desire. For me.

"*Evan.*"

With her fingers wrapped around my wrist, she digs her nails into the skin slightly as I press one finger inside her.

"So fucking wet for me. Are you ready for me to fill you up with my cock?"

"Now," she whimpers.

I shift until I'm between her thighs and slide slowly into her in one long thrust that leaves us both moaning.

"This is exactly what I needed. You wrapped around my dick, gripping me like a goddamn vise. Fuck. Best fucking Christmas present ever."

She tips her head back, exposing her neck to me, and I nip at the tendon on display.

"*Yes!*"

"Tell me you feel this too, princess. Tell me I'm not alone."

I trail kisses along her throat, stopping at the pulse beating wildly beneath her skin.

"You're not alone. I feel it, Evan. I feel it."

Her hands on my back, she clutches me to her as I piston my hips against hers, picking up speed while the orgasm builds exponentially in my spine.

"I'm not giving you up, Lilah. Not for Cornerstone, not for anything. You're mine."

"Yours," she moans. "And you're mine."

She lifts her head, her lips finding mine, and our tongues tangle as the orgasm takes over the movement of my body, building and cresting in a massive explosion of white light. I shout my release as I pour myself into her, sealing the reality I've known for a long time but still can't admit out loud.

I love Lilah Stevens.

CHAPTER 10

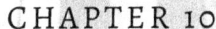

LILAH

I stretch across the bed, searching for Evan—
something I found myself doing several times
throughout the night—the soreness of my muscles serve as a
reminder of how each time we came together through the
night was just as explosive as the first time. But also more.
More connection, more emotion, more…

Love?

No. It can't be. We only came clean about not hating each
other a week ago. And, sure, we've spent almost all our days
and nights together since then, but love? It's too soon. Even if
the warmth blooming in my chest where my heart beats calls
me out.

Liar, liar, pants on fire.

My hand drifts to the cool sheets of the bed instead of
encountering the warm body I'm intimately familiar with.

I lift my head. "Evan?"

My voice is hoarse and rough to my own ears, and I
wince and clear my throat before my attention catches on
the spare notebook from my kitchen that's now sitting on
the nightstand on his side of the bed.

Princess,

You have no idea how hard it was to drag my sorry ass out of bed and not wake you up with my dick sheathed in that sweet little pussy. Later. ;) But I had to take care of something important this morning and didn't have the heart to wake you. I'll be back later and will tell you more then.

Evan.

How can a handful of lines scribbled almost illegibly across the page contain so much dirty talk along with the sweetest sentiments? Dropping my head to his pillow, I breathe deeply, catching notes of his scent—the blend of citrus and spices is uniquely him. My need for him swamps me, and I groan.

Whatever he's doing must be important if it pulled him from me without even a goodbye. He said he'd tell me later, so whatever it is isn't a secret. But what on earth would drag him out after only a few hours of sleep?

My phone buzzes on my nightstand, and I roll over, clutching Evan's pillow to my chest, and pick it up. There's a message in the band's group text.

CHRIS

We have a meeting at Cornerstone in two hours.

FINN

thumbs up emoji

MILO

2 hours? Why?

CHRIS

We nee to talk.

MILO

About what?

CHRIS

Milo, just be here in two hours, okay?

FINN

Fine.

I'll be there.

Evan doesn't respond right away, so I send him a separate one to make sure he sees the group thread.

Don't want to interrupt, but I wanted to make sure you got the text about the meeting.

EVAN

I did, princess. Thanks. I'll see you there.

It gives me no clue as to where he is right now, but at least his response is reassuring. I'll see him again in a couple of hours.

Girl, you've got it bad.

"Shut up," I say aloud and toss back the covers. I need to get ready.

One look in the mirror tells me I can't lie to myself. So how can I hide it from Evan and the guys?

I'm in love with Evan Andrews, and the truth is written all over my face.

🎹 🎹 🎹

"Milo, I can't. You know that." Chloe sounds close to tears

when I open the conference room door almost two hours later.

"Chloe—" Milo cuts off as soon as he sees me, and when Chloe follows his gaze, she stiffens before pushing back from the table to rush past me.

"Sorry. I didn't mean to interrupt…" I seriously wish I hadn't walked in when I did, but I'm looking for Evan. I haven't heard from him since my text earlier, and this pit in my stomach won't go away.

I want Evan to wrap me in his arms and tell me everything will be okay. And I'm not *that* girl, so the desire to find him for a hug is new to me. Is this what love is like? If so, then I have a bone to pick with Cupid.

Milo drags a hand through his much shorter—which is still shocking—hair.

"You didn't. Not really." He looks so forlorn that his heartbreak is like another person in the room with us.

"What's going on?" I ask, sitting in the chair Chloe vacated a few minutes ago.

"I…nothing."

"That didn't look like nothing."

He sighs, and the silence draws out for so long I'm convinced he's not going to answer me.

"How did Evan convince you to give him a chance?"

His question catches me off guard.

"Huh?"

"What made you decide you didn't hate him?"

"I-I never hated him," I admit. Even at his hottest and coldest, I was confused, but that puzzlement stemmed from a combination of attraction and my inability to explain why he reacted to me the way he did.

"You didn't?"

"No. I thought he hated me."

"Nah. If he hated you, he would have vetoed the decision to bring you on board."

"What?"

"We voted. It's the way we've done things since we were in high school. Evan wasn't happy about the vote, but he didn't say no. He wanted you around, I think."

Knowing he wanted me, even if it was begrudgingly at first, creates a fizzling warmth in my blood.

"Oh."

"You've been good for him, Lilah. He's...he's more alive than I've seen him in years, if that makes sense. He was going through the motions, but like it was muscle memory and not because he wanted to. It was like he was playing a part versus doing what he loved. What we all love."

"Aww, Milo." I rub a hand up and down his arm. "You really are a romantic, aren't you?"

"Think you could tell Chloe that? Maybe that'll give me a chance with her."

"Chloe?" I guess my suspicion about him having a crush on her was right, but I'm not sure she sees him the same way.

Our publicist is four years younger than I am, which makes her nine years younger than our drummer.

"Is Chloe who you've been talking about for the last few months?" I ask.

He nods, looking more solemn than I think I've ever seen him.

"And your hair?"

His sheepish grin is answer enough, but he nods again. "Yeah. I figured maybe if I showed her I was serious, she would give me a chance. I want to be different. For her."

"Short hair doesn't make you serious."

He snorts a laugh. "She said something similar."

"Maybe you need to be her friend. Only her friend."

The despondent look in his eyes when he glances up pierces my heart, and I blink back tears.

"I don't know if I can."

"Aww." I don't hesitate to wrap my arms around him and pull him into a hug.

"I thought mistletoe was for kissing." Finn's voice breaks into the conversation, and both Milo and I glance up to see the little sprig hung above the table.

"What in the world?" I ask. Surely this is some sort of sexual harassment suit waiting to happen.

"Christmas party was last night," Finn says with a shrug. "Probably leftover from that."

Milo looks at me, the semi-goofy playboy persona locked in place instead of the thoughtful, emotional person I was just talking to.

"What do you say, Lil? Want to experience kissing the tongue master?"

I roll my eyes, not fighting the giggle that bubbles up. "I've already experienced kissing the tongue master. And that's not you. Not by a long shot, big talker."

He puckers up, smacking his lips together. "Come get it, beautiful."

I lean forward, pressing my lips against his playfully. The mistletoe above us demands it.

"*What the fuck?*"

I spring back at the hurt permeating Evan's voice. He's standing inside the conference room door, the betrayal written all over his face quickly being replaced by a rolling storm of anger, obliterating the hurt.

"Evan—" Chris wraps his fingers around Evan's bicep, but he shrugs out of the hold.

"What the fuck is this?" he asks, stalking forward. He's close enough to touch, but I keep my hands firmly in my lap.

"I—"

"Ev—"

"It's—"

Finn, Milo, and I all talk at once but fall silent and awkwardly wait for one of the others to take over.

Clearing my throat, I try again. "It's nothing. Just a mistletoe k—"

"It didn't fucking look like nothing, *princess*." The nickname had finally grown on me, but I hate the way he hurls it in my direction now.

But he isn't finished.

"What? One member of JOY not enough for you? You need to fuck around with Milo too? Or was it Milo and Finn together? Does the thought of fucking two guys at once do it for you?" he sneers.

Oh no, he fucking didn't.

"Excuse me?" I rise from the chair, refusing to let him look down at me. It doesn't fix the situation since he's still taller than I am, but at least now he doesn't tower over me.

His nostrils flare.

"My dick not enough for you, Lilah? You want Milo too?"

"Evan. It's not like that, bro. Look up." Finn points to the ceiling, but Evan doesn't spare the innocent-looking plant a glance.

"How long has this shit been going on?" he fumes.

"Nothing is going on." I'm surprised by how calm I sound, given how pissed I am at him and his asshole assumptions.

"Kissing my bandmate isn't fucking nothing."

"Dude, chill out—" Milo's message is cut off by Evan's punch to the face. "What the fuck?" Milo covers his bleeding nose while Chris rushes forward and steps between them.

"Enough." He glares at Evan and then at Milo. "Milo, go clean up. Finn, help Milo."

Once the two of them leave, Evan's energy flags, and he drops into the chair Milo was sitting in earlier.

"What the fuck?" Chris asks.

"Again. He did it again. He promised he wouldn't. He swore the first time was an accident…" Evan's words trail off and leave me more confused than before.

What the fuck is he talking about?

"Ev, you don't—"

"Fuck this. I never should have done this. I'm out of here." As quickly as he sat, he surges up, brushing past me and slamming out of the room before I can stop him.

Chris sighs and stands. "Lilah."

Why is he surprised I'm still here?

"What the hell was all that about?"

"Noth—"

"And don't you dare give me that bullshit." I cross my arms and stare at the bassist. "Friends don't punch friends for nothing."

"It's not my story to tell."

"Well, you're the only one here right now."

He shakes his head. "You need to ask Evan."

"I doubt he's fucking speaking to me right now."

Asshole. Screw him. *I'm* not speaking to *him*.

"Just give him time."

I throw my hands up with a growl. "That's been your advice for months, Chris. Six fucking months of 'give him time' and 'he'll come around.' And where are we now? Six months down the road, and I'm still in the same boat I was on that first day."

But worse. Like that boat's sinking and taking me down with it, because I know who Evan is now. The real Evan and not the asshole he pretended to be for so long. I'm in lo— Shit. I can't go back to dealing with Asshole Andrews.

"If that asshole comes back, tell him he can come find me when he's ready to explain his behavior. I'll see if I'm ready to listen." I spin and head for the door, exhausted from the whiplash I've experienced over the last twenty minutes.

I ignore Chris's request to stop and skirt the bathroom where I assume Finn is helping Milo clean up.

I'd give anything to wake up in bed next to Evan and discover this was all a bad dream.

But Santa doesn't give presents to girls who claim their coal.

And it's time I accepted that fact.

CHAPTER 11

EVAN

"*W*here the fuck are you, you jackass?" Chris's voice echoes through the entryway of my house. I never should have given him the code to my door.

But we've been best friends since we were eleven, so he has my shit like I have his shit. There's no hiding. Even when I want to.

I don't respond from my prone position on the couch, but the bastard has a sixth sense and steps into the dimly lit room like I have a homing beacon implanted in my ass.

"Have you been lying here in the dark like a damn vampire since you left Cornerstone?"

I grunt and pop one eye open, following his movements as he makes his way to the windows and cursing when he throws open the curtains and bright sunlight streams in.

"*Fuck.* No, I haven't been lying here since I got home." My discarded guitar next to me should prove my point.

But everything I tried to play had Lilah's voice drilling into my head like a goddamn woodpecker. Her soft alto skimming notes written only for her, weaving itself into the melody moving from my head to my fingers.

"You writing?" Chris nods to the pen and paper I never got out of the habit of having nearby. The pen scratching against the paper is part of my creative process.

"Maybe." Snatches of music keep floating in and out of my mind, but nothing has made it onto the scribbled page.

"Been a while."

He and I both remember the last time I wrote—the day after I caught my newly ex-girlfriend in Milo's bed. My first reaction had been to punch him. Turns out, I should have asked questions.

Exactly what I did today. But this is different. It was obvious once I calmed down and stopped letting the past collide with the present.

"Before you say anything else, I know I fucked up," I say, moving until I can sit up on the couch with my elbows resting on my knees.

"Exactly how do you think you fucked up today?" Chris asks.

I groan. Father Chris came to hear my confession.

"I shouldn't have punched Milo. The asshole may deserve it most of the time, but not today."

"No, not today."

"What? What do you know that I don't?" Because after almost thirty years, his tone tells me more than his words.

"Milo isn't interested in Lilah—"

"He flirts with her all the fucking time. Tell me another fairy tale."

"How about the one where Milo and Chloe slept together in San Francisco?"

It takes a minute for his words to sink in.

"Milo and Chloe what? Didn't she just graduate from college? Fuck, is she even old enough to drink?"

Chris winces. Probably because of the thirteen-year age gap between Jessie and him.

"I mean, didn't we already tell him Cornerstone employees were off-limits? Again?" Because of course Milo would need more than one warning not to fuck with women who work for our label. It was obvious to all of us the day Chloe was introduced.

Hence the—ignored—reminder.

He shrugs. "He says she's different. She's the girl he's been talking about for the last few months. The reason he doesn't go out anymore, the reason he cut his hair. Apparently, she told him the day before the concert that she didn't find long hair on guys attractive."

Milo's haircut threw us all. The man has had a man bun since before they were popular. Then, the night of the concert, he walked in with his neck on display for the first time since, well, ever.

"He did that for her?"

Chris nods. "Supposedly."

"Fuck. I guess I owe that asshole an apology, then." I already knew that, but to admit it out loud sticks slightly.

"He's not the only one you owe an apology."

Lilah.

I drop my head into my hands, my focus trained on the pattern of the rug under my toes.

"She's not Taylor."

My head snaps up, my gaze colliding with his.

"I fucking know she's not Taylor."

My ex-girlfriend roofied one of my best friends and pretended to sleep with him, all because I broke up with her. I was her free entry into the hottest industry parties and the platinum credit card she used at all her favorite stores—and those weren't Target or H&M.

"Fuck," I groan and collapse back against the pillows. "How pissed is she?"

"Scale of one to ten?"

"Yeah."

"Fifty."

"*Fuck*."

"You pretty much called her a whore, Ev."

"I know." I rise from the couch and pace a small square in my living room.

"Accused her of cheating on you."

"I know."

"Then walked out of the room after you decked Milo. Brushed past her like she wasn't there."

"*I know*. Okay? I know!"

"So what the fuck are you going to do about it?"

His question has me stopping short.

"Apologize."

"And?"

"And what? I'm going to apologize."

"You can't just apologize."

"What do you mean I can't just apologize?"

Chris rolls his eyes like he's talking to his five-year-old midtantrum.

"You need to grovel."

"Huh?"

"You need to do more than apologize, and you need to mean it. Tell her how you feel about her."

"She knows how I feel about her."

"You've told her you love her?"

"Not exactly," I mumble.

"Not exactly?" His eyebrows shoot to his hairline.

"Not yet."

"What the fuck are you waiting for?"

"I've barely figured it out myself. How the hell did you know?"

"Everyone does."

"*What?*"

Seriously?

"Except for Lilah," Milo says, stepping into the living room with Finn on his heels.

"When the fuck did you get here?"

He grabs a chip out of the bag in his arm—apparently, he and Finn raided my kitchen—and scrutinizes me. Fortunately, my hit didn't do much damage.

"I brought them," Chris says.

"So you can apologize to me," Milo chimes in, shoving a handful of chips into his mouth.

"Didn't your mother ever tell you not to talk with your mouth full?"

"No, but yours did." He smirks.

He's right. It was a phrase she said often around the five of us anytime we hung out at my house.

I sigh as guilt swamps me. I punched one of my best friends—one of my brothers—before stopping to ask questions.

"Fuck, Mi, I'm—"

"Forget it." He waves away my apology before I can get it all the way out. "Already forgotten, bro."

I reach out a hand, and he clasps it, yanking me into a bruising hug. Fucker is strong from hours spent with his drums.

"Aww," Chris and Finn chime in from around us, and both Milo and I flip them the bird.

"Now that that's settled, we need a plan," Milo says, pulling away.

"A plan?"

"We're gonna win you back your girl, Andrews."

"What about you?" I ask.

He shrugs. "You first."

CHAPTER 12

LILAH

*M*y phone vibrates in my lap.

Mother.

Probably wondering where I am since her last edict, the one that came two days ago, was for me to arrive for Christmas Eve festivities promptly at three. And it's now 3:03, according to the digital readout on my lock screen.

Heaving a massive sigh, I accept the call.

"Hello?"

"Are you on your way?"

No hello back, no other greeting. Straight to the point, with a tone full of disappointment.

"No."

"No?"

How many people dare tell her *no*?

"I never said I was coming."

She's silent. Probably working on her gaslighting technique. Contemplating which way she can convince me that I *did* agree.

"Everyone is expecting you to be here," she finally says.

Of course. Because image is everything.

"I'm not."

"Lilah, I don't know how much longer your father and I can put up with your quarter-life crisis or whatever you want to call this little rebellion you've staged in recent years."

My back teeth grind together.

"Mother, I am not experiencing any sort of life crisis." Even if I am experiencing a broken heart. "Furthermore, my being in the band is not a rebellion. This is my job. My dream job at that."

She scoffs. "You don't need to work. Why can't you be more like your sisters?"

"I know I don't need to work. I *get* to."

"You're exactly like your Aunt Sarah."

It's the best compliment she's ever paid me.

"Thank you."

"Now that I know you're not lying dead in a ditch somewhere, I have to get ready. Lara and Leighton will be here soon."

At least my mother can console herself with my younger sisters.

"Okay, please tell everyone I said Merry Christmas."

The only response is the click of the phone.

At least now I have confirmation that my phone does indeed work. Wouldn't know it by how often it *hasn't* rung in the last two days.

Not like I want to talk to anyone.

That's a lie.

I want to talk to Evan. The blow-up in the conference room was two days ago. For the first twenty-four hours, I had this vision in my head. One where he would show up at my door and apologize. Sort of like John Cusack in *Say Anything.* The next twelve hours were spent waiting for a phone call I assumed was coming, even if it was to tell me we were through but that I was still a member of the band and we could be civil to each other.

For the last twelve hours, I've alternated between rage-cleaning my apartment and watching the two Hollie Berry Christmas movies I have on DVD. *All Snowed Inn* is currently cycling through the credits.

"Time to watch *Chasing Snowflakes* again. Is three times too many?" I snort. "Great, Lilah, just great. Talking to yourself. Maybe you should avoid cutesy holiday romances from now on and stick to classics like *Die Hard*. At least John McClane had Al to talk to when he was on his own."

And sure, there are people I can call. But it's Christmas Eve. Everyone is busy celebrating the holiday with their loved ones. Eating a fabulous dinner they spent all day preparing instead of falling face first into a giant bowl of popcorn.

My phone vibrates again, and this time, I'm equal parts hopeful it's Evan and fearful of my mother calling back.

Aunt Sarah.

Visiting her in Montana for Christmas sounds better than what I'm doing now.

"Hello?"

"Merry Christmas, my little lilac tree."

My lips curve slightly for the first time since I walked out of the conference room at Cornerstone. Her greeting never fails to do that. I've been Aunt Sarah's lilac tree for as long as I can remember.

"You too. How's your white Christmas?"

Every year, she reminds me that I'll only get a white Christmas if I come to see her.

"Can't really say it's white unless I count the sand on the beaches."

"Beaches? You're not in Montana?"

Her tinkling laughter sounds far away. "No, I didn't want to tromp through however many feet of snow for the holidays this year. I'm in the Virgin Islands, checking out a resort some friends were telling me about—the Indigo Royal."

"Oh yeah?"

"It's this great resort on St. Thomas. All sorts of eighties music references. And the food...I've probably gained ten pounds in the two days I've been here."

Two days. I swallow painfully at the reminder. It stings, even though it has nothing to do with my situation.

"So you're there for Christmas?"

"And New Year's. Who knows, I may stay down here a while. I'm tired of cold weather."

"But what about your digs? Your friends? Your students?"

"My house isn't for sale yet, lilac tree. I'm only thinking about it. Have to wait for the snow to melt for my next dig anyway. Not like all of this is happening tomorrow."

"Oh."

"You can visit me here, same as you could in Montana. Maybe more often since the weather is nicer."

"Yeah, I know."

"Something the matter?"

"No."

"Are you hiding from your parents' latest choice of suitor?"

I shudder at the image of yet another corporate yuppie they probably had lined up to introduce me to at their holiday party.

"I didn't go. Mom called when I didn't show up at the appointed time. She wants to know why I can't be more like Lara and Leighton."

"Because you're not a Stepford clone."

I giggle. "Neither are you."

"No, neither of us is interested in pearls and peonies."

"How did we end up so different?"

"I'd like to say I know, lilac tree. But the truth is, I've been asking myself that question since your mom and I were kids."

"Figured out any answers?"

"Not really. But I've realized that just because they're family doesn't mean they understand us. Friends though. Friends are the family we choose."

The guys are my family. Milo. Finn. Chris.

Evan.

The lump in my throat is back. The one I've refused to acknowledge before now.

"Doing something with the guys for the holiday?" she asks.

"Nah. Just watching Hollie Berry movies."

"Hollie Berry, huh? She's been all over the gossip magazines recently, hasn't she? Something about claiming her coal?"

"Yeah. Being independent. Her own woman. Not taking shit from anyone."

"Sounds like my kind of girl. Reminds me of you."

My laughter is self-deprecating. "I wish."

"You want to talk about it?" she asks.

"About what?"

"What's bugging you. I may not be able to see you, but I can hear it in your voice. You're upset."

I blink rapidly at the tears gathering along my lashes, feeling lonelier than I did even a few minutes ago. "There's not much to talk about."

Because I still haven't figured out what exactly Evan and I had and how it got so screwed up so fast.

"You want to come down and join me for New Year's?"

"I'll think about it—" My interior phone buzzes then. The

one connected to the front desk of the building, so I hastily say goodbye and snatch it off the receiver.

"Yes?"

"Princess."

The tears are back with a vengeance, but I can't tell whether they're angry tears or sad tears. Evan's voice was the last one I expected when I picked up this phone.

"Go away, Evan."

"I want to talk to you. Please. Just give me a few minutes. I called from down here because I didn't want to just show up at your door unannounced if you didn't want to see me. I don't want to take that choice away from you."

"I have nothing to say to you."

"I have some stuff to tell you. Please? Five minutes. If you still want me to go after that, I'll leave."

I hesitate. Stupid heart. The tone of his voice when he uses the word *please* sways the traitorous organ.

"I shouldn't—"

"I'll be right there."

The line goes dead, and my heart pounds in my chest.

I don't want to see him.

I need to see him.

What could he possibly say to make up for the accusations he slung in my direction?

A soft knock signals that my time for contemplation is up. Taking a deep breath, I square my shoulders and open the door immediately so he knows where I am—right on the other side.

Scruff shadows his normally sharp jawline, and dark smudges are evident beneath eyes the color of a stormy ocean. I want to move closer and wrap my arms around him.

The fuck you do. We're mad at him, remember?

I straighten, steel infusing my spine and locking me in place with my hand on the door.

"Princess—"

"What do you want, Evan?" At least my voice is strong. But I'm sure my oversized sweatshirt and yoga pants, lack of makeup, and the messy bun on top of my head counteract the effect.

His shoulders sink, and his eyes lose what little light had filtered from inside the depths.

"I wanted to apologize."

Words I wanted to hear. So why don't they fix me?

"I was wrong," he goes on when I simply continue to stare at him.

"You're damn right you were wrong."

I hold steady when he reaches for me, not willing to simply forgive and forget.

"Lilah." The pleading note to his voice, coupled with the sheer regret on his face, has my defenses crumbling faster than a sandcastle at high tide.

"Evan."

"Can I come in?"

"I don't think that's a good idea."

Because I will cave. And if I cave now, it tells him his behavior two days ago was okay when it was anything but. I was...whatever we were doing *with him*. Only him.

He sighs. "That's fair. I'm sorry. I fucked up. Accusing you the way I did and going at Milo like that…"

"What the hell possessed you to react that way? Milo and I are friends. Only friends."

"I know that when I think about it rationally. But walking in like that, it reminded me of my past—"

"I have nothing to do with that," I snap, because I still have no fucking clue what happened.

"I didn't say that." His voice holds the hint of an argument for the first time since he showed up here.

"What are you saying? Because other than the apology,

that's all I'm hearing. And I'm not the only one you should be apologizing to."

"Fuck this." Between one breath and the next, he closes the distance between us and yanks me into his arms. "I'm saying I love you."

His words hold me motionless in his arms.

"What?"

His grip loosens, but I still don't move out of his hold.

"I love you. I've loved you since the first time I saw you in that audition room. You were so goddamned focused on getting the keyboard settings just right." His lips quirk in a slight smile. "I loved you even though I was terrified of everything I felt for you. My last girlfriend turned into someone I didn't like. All she cared about was status and money. And then she became someone I despised. When I broke up with her, she roofied one of my best friends and made me think the two of them had sex."

"That's why you hit Milo?"

He nods. "The fucker more often than not deserves to be slapped upside the head, but I know deep down he's not a bad guy. He just irritates me."

"I noticed."

"I hated how easy you were with him. How the two of you hit it off so fast—"

"As friends. Milo and I are just friends. He's like my annoying big brother. He and Finn and Chris...none of them are you."

"They're a whole lot nicer than I am."

I trail both hands up his chest to his jaw, cupping it, soaking in the warmth that surges in a wave through my body when his eyes close and tension releases from him.

"They're not you. I don't feel about them the way I do about you."

Bright-blue eyes pop open and lock on mine.

"How do you feel about me?"

"Fifteen minutes ago, I wanted to strangle you. What you said hurt, Evan. A lot."

A frown forms between his eyebrows.

"I'm sorry. I—I can't think straight where you're concerned."

"Well, you need to get something through your skull."

"What?" he asks.

"You're who I want to be with. Not Milo. Not Finn. Not Chris or anyone else who comes along. You. And when I'm with you, I'm *with* you. No one else enters my head. But if you think you have an easy excuse to act the way you did again, you're going to need to learn that's not okay with me."

"I promise. Never again." He pulls me close enough that his heart beats against mine. "I don't want to lose you."

"I'm not going anywhere," I tell him and bring my lips close to his ear. "I love you too."

The words are barely past my lips when his mouth claims mine in a kiss that curls my toes and has me clinging to him by the time he lifts his head.

"What was that?" he asks, glancing over my shoulder while he walks me back into my apartment.

"What was what?" I ask, looking behind me. All I see are the home screen of the movie and the brightly lit Christmas tree.

"Santa." His breath tickles my ear.

"Santa, huh?" I giggle.

"Did he bring you what you wanted, princess?" He flexes his hands against my hips.

"No. He brought me something better. Something I accidentally left off my Christmas list."

"Yeah?" The devilish smirk on his face has my insides quivering with need.

"Coal."

"Coal?"

"After all, I'm not on Santa's nice list."

"You're saying you're naughty?"

"Why don't you kiss me again and find out?" I challenge.

Turns out we're both on Santa's naughty list this year. And there's nowhere else I'd rather be.

CHAPTER 13

EVAN

*C*licking *End* on my call with Chris, I leave my bedroom in search of Lilah.

My New Year's Eve plans are centered on one thing only —making love to my girlfriend.

Girlfriend.

It's such a junior high word.

But *love of my life* sounds too fucking sappy.

"Princess?"

I shouldn't have let Chris's call distract me from the perfection of Lilah's body on the bed. But I've been waiting on this call since he rescheduled the meeting with Cornerstone. Now, not only do I want to pick up where Lilah and I left off, but I have news.

Not finding her upstairs, I head down, following the humming audible from the kitchen where she bounces around, putting together a tray of snacks and champagne glasses.

I lean against the counter and silently take in the show. The shake of her ass under the thin white T-shirt of mine she's wearing. The creamy expanse of thigh disappearing beneath the hem. The memory of exactly what's under it—nothing.

My dick kicks against the cotton of my sweats, ready to pick up where we left off upstairs. I heave myself away from the counter and line my body up behind Lilah's, my hands finding her hips under the shirt.

"Jesus." She jumps but relaxes against me immediately. "You scared me. I thought you were still on the phone with Chris."

"All done," I murmur, tracing her exposed neck up to her ear with my lips.

She tilts her head, granting me enough access to nip at the tendon before soothing the mark with my tongue.

"Mmm." Arching her back, she presses her ass against my dick.

"Want to know what he had to say?" I smooth my hands along the soft skin of her stomach and cup her breasts, tweaking her nipples with my thumbs and forefingers.

"*Yes.*"

"Pay attention, princess." I work one nipple while I slide my other hand back down. My fingers glide through her folds until I find the hard nub begging for my attention.

Her legs buckle, and I press her closer to the counter to hold her up.

"*Evan.*" Her plea ends on a gasp as I trace a circle around her clit.

"Are you listening? Or are you too focused on what my fingers are doing to you?" I simultaneously pinch her clit and her nipple, loving the way my name breaks on her lips.

"I-I-I'm listening."

"As of today, Just One Yesterday is no longer with Cornerstone."

She tenses and her head whips around, her desire

dimmed at my announcement. I take advantage, claiming her lips with mine.

"Wait, wait, wait," she says after breaking the kiss. "You can't just say that and not explain. What happened?"

She turns, dislodging my hands and crossing her arms over her chest. "Explain."

"You're adorable when you glare," I tell her and wrap my arms around her again so I can squeeze her ass.

"Stop that and explain."

"Chris and I have been talking a lot about labels. Cornerstone has changed so much over the years. First with all their shit with Noah and then the no-frat clause. It was going to be a battle for me to be with you."

"So you left your label for me? What does that mean?"

"We'll get everyone together after the new year and talk about Chris's suggestion. Arrhythmic is family, so we think they'd be a good fit. You're important to me. I told you once —I'm not letting you go. Not for anything or anyone. I love you."

Her gaze softens with my words.

"I love you."

She rises to her tiptoes and tugs on my neck so she can seal her lips to mine, her tongue almost immediately seeking entrance to tango with mine while her fingernails scratch down my back and under the waistband of my sweats.

I rest my hands at her hips and boost her to the counter. Something drops to the floor, but neither of us breaks the kiss to find out what it is, too caught up in each other to think about anything but getting fingers and lips on skin. Lilah wraps her legs around my hips, pushing my sweats down until my cock springs free.

She wraps her fingers around my swollen length and tugs until I release her lips with a groan.

"Fuck, princess."

I barely manage to whip the T-shirt she's wearing over her head before my lips are on her neck again, resting against the pulse that flutters rapidly at the base.

"That's exactly what I want you to do," she murmurs before she nips my ear.

My hips jerk involuntarily, but I leash the desire pulsing through my veins. Otherwise, this will be over before it's fully begun. I drop my head, capturing a dusky-pink nipple and sinking my teeth into it roughly.

She cries out, threading her fingers through my hair and holding me to her so I repeat the rough caress.

"You like my teeth marking you, princess? Making you mine? I don't need to fuck you"—I grip her ass and pull her tighter to me—"but I'm going to drive my cock so deep inside you that you won't know where you end and I begin."

I glide my index finger down between her breasts and over her belly button, finally coming to a stop between her thighs.

"Fuck, you're soaked. Ready for me. You want me to take you right here?"

She nods. "Yes. Now. Please."

"Please, huh? Please what? Please, this?" I switch from one breast to the next, swirling the stiff peak in my mouth and twisting my fingers around the now abandoned one.

Her hips buck off the counter, desire coating my finger where it circles her clit slowly.

She mewls, and I shift until I can press my finger knuckle deep into her pussy.

"Or this? Do you like my finger here and my thumb at your clit? Is this what you want?"

"No."

"No?" I push forward with my finger and retreat, slowly at first, and gaining momentum until she's writhing between me and the counter.

"I...want...you." Her words are pants while her fingernails dig into the backs of my biceps.

"You have me." I stroke my finger slowly against her to prove my point.

"Your dick."

"Where do you want it, princess?"

"Evan." Her whine turns to a moan when I replace my finger with my dick, pressing forward until I'm seated all the way inside her.

Her walls flutter around me, and I grip her hips. I retreat until her legs lock in place, her feet pressing against my ass to push me forward again.

Keeping one hand in place, I move my other between us, dragging my finger around her clit, reveling in the way her walls grip my dick like a vise. I don't let up on the steady rotations, adding slight pressure every now and then to keep her orgasm building but not cresting.

"Help me," I grind out, my own orgasm pulsing through my spine and gathering in my balls.

Her eyes flutter open.

"Touch yourself. Your breasts," I clarify, following the movement of her hands as she brings them up to tweak her nipples, and her pussy tightens again. "Harder. Harder."

My vision tunnels as the grip around my dick intensifies and her breathing grows more ragged. Every muscle in her legs locks around me as her orgasm hits her with full force.

"Evan. Oh god. Oh my...I love you." Her rhythm falters as pleasure overtakes her body.

"I love you. I love you. I. love. you." I can no longer deny the need to come, the orgasm overwhelming me in an experience guaranteed to send me into orbit while grounding me right here. Right now. With Lilah.

She is my center.

When I come back to earth, her nails scratch lightly along

my back and her lips are pressed against the pulse point in my throat.

"Happy New Year, baby," she whispers to me.

"Happy New Year, princess."

The first of many more to come.

EPILOGUE

EVAN

1 YEAR LATER

The effervescent happiness on Lilah's face makes the last two days of freezing temperatures worth it. So I push aside all thoughts about how I can't feel my toes despite the socks that swore to keep them nice and toasty. Instead, I focus on what she's saying when we step into the cabin.

"Lumi was probably my favorite, but I love the way Kaisla wouldn't leave Joona alone."

We spent today with several husky teams, and every dog seemed to fall in love with Lilah—which isn't hard to do. But I can see where this is going.

"You're not getting a team of huskies when we go home. We don't need dog sleds in LA."

Her lower lip protrudes, and I lean forward and nip at the plump flesh, earning me a jump and a squeak, then a longer brush of our lips.

"Not a team, no. But wouldn't one be fun? Well, two, so they're not lonely."

"Princess, we're not going to be home much for six months. A tour bus probably isn't the best place for a puppy."

"Two puppies."

"Definitely not, then."

"Fine. But after we get home, we're talking about this again."

"Whatever you want, baby."

Because it's true. If she wants two puppies—fuck, if she wants a hundred and one—if it makes her happy, I'll do it.

She drops her coat on the couch and stops, looking at the bed and then into the glass enclosed igloo structure at the end of the cabin. Since we've been here, it's housed two cots for viewing the northern lights. But this morning while she was in the shower, I called and asked for a different setup.

Now it boasts a stack of blankets and pillows, with a bottle of champagne on ice.

"What in the...did you do this?"

"Not me exactly." I wink. "I've been with you all day. But I thought it would be fun to check out the lights like this tonight."

She moves closer, twisting her fingers in my shirt and tugging until she presses her lips against mine.

"You really are the sweetest, aren't you?"

"You're only now realizing this?"

It's been just over a year since we first got together, but a year ago today, I pulled my head out of my ass and told her how much I loved her. How I would battle anyone and anything to keep her in my life. A year of gossip as news broke that we had left Cornerstone and moved to Arrhythmic. A year of settling in at our new label and with each other.

"No." She shakes her head and brushes her lips teasingly

against mine until I stop her with both hands on her cheeks and deepen the kiss. The tastes of chocolate, mint, and cold air greet my tongue, and I can't stop the shiver as I break the kiss.

"Still cold?" She rubs my arms roughly, trying to warm me up.

I grin. "I think I forgot what warmth feels like."

"Maybe we need to share body heat," she suggests, making my dick harden in a painful rush.

Not yet.

"And what is Santa going to say when we visit him tomorrow?"

Santa's house is set up here at the resort. Supposedly, the real Santa was from here hundreds of years ago, and the tribe, the Sami, were his "elves."

"Aren't we a little old to visit Santa?"

"Blasphemy," I tease. "We're in his hometown. Of course we need to visit him."

"I don't intend to land on his nice list tonight. It's a little late for that." With one hand, she cups me through my thick pants. "You're wearing too many clothes."

I grit my teeth as the temptation to toss her onto the pile of blankets grows stronger. Instead, I pry her hand loose and press a kiss roughly against her palm.

"Let's watch the lights first."

This might be the first time I've suggested something other than immediately moving our foreplay to more. Her confusion is evident in the wrinkle between her eyebrows, and I press my lips there, breathing in her unique scent coupled with the freshness of the air and snow.

"*Okay...*"

"Why don't we get changed, and I'll meet you in there?" I motion to the glass igloo.

She nods before disappearing into the bathroom.

I double-check that everything is ready before rushing into a pair of flannel pants, opting to keep my thermal shirt on. I've just uncorked the champagne when she leaves the bathroom, her own thermals still in place.

Maybe I should have opted for a warmer locale for Christmas. Somewhere she could walk toward me naked. But I know how much my girl loves the idea of a white Christmas. It may not snow here tomorrow, but there's plenty of the frozen stuff as far as the eye can see.

"Champagne?" I ask once she's folded herself gracefully to the floor.

Nerves assault my stomach. *Is now the right time for this?* But I shake off the anxiety. I can't imagine a better moment.

She takes a sip before setting the flute off to the side and lying back to stare through the glass at the rainbows of lights already visible around us.

"This is so magical. Thank you for bringing me here."

"You're welcome. Were you really surprised?"

She tilts her head, and her eyes meet mine in the dim light. "I was. This has been amazing."

Unable to resist, I angle closer and tease her lips with a chaste kiss. "I love you."

She gives me a soft smile. "I love you too. Aren't you going to look at the lights?"

"In a minute."

The look she gives me is quizzical—furrowed brow, slight frown. "What are you up to, Andrews?"

My palms grow clammy where they rest against the blanket, and I can't help but smile. Damn, she's gorgeous. "Nothing."

"The last time you had that look on your face and said 'nothing' was right before you went down on me in the recording booth."

It was during a session for our new album. She was

supposed to be in her booth and me in mine. Instead, I snuck into her booth and didn't stop until she was begging me to take her home. We made it as far as the car in the parking garage.

"We're not in a recording booth," I remind her.

Her eyes glaze over and her tongue peeks out to moisten her lips. Suddenly, I wish we were.

Focus.

"I love you," I tell her again. I'll never tire of those words.

Her face softens. "I love you too."

"I'm never going to stop either. It's been a crazy year. The label shifting and recording and everything—"

"And moving in with you," she adds.

"The only constant has been how much I love you. How much it grows every day. You moving in with me was one of the highlights of my year. I love waking up with you next to me."

"Just *one* of your highlights?" She pouts. "What was better than that?"

"It hasn't happened yet."

"So how do you know that'll be your favorite?" she asks.

"I don't. That's up to you. And what you say."

"To what?"

Tugging the small box out from under one of the blankets where I've hidden it, I swallow hard, then open it and show her the princess-cut diamond ring cushioned along the black velvet. The band is my favorite part. It's an infinity twist of white gold and more diamonds.

Her breath catches, and her eyes shoot from the ring in my hand to my eyes.

"Lilah Julianne Stevens, the last eighteen months has been the best of my life. Not only did we find our new keyboardist, but my heart found its other half. I called your aunt last month and asked her what she thought about my asking you this question. And while she gave me her whole-hearted blessing, she said you were woman enough to make up your own mind. Last year, you claimed your coal, and this year, I hope you'll let me claim you for my wife. Will you marry me?"

She launches herself at me, arms wrapping around my neck while her muffled yeses press against my lips. Her lips taste sweeter each time I kiss her.

I pull back long enough to slide the ring on her finger and admire the sparkle in the inky darkness. Rainbows flash at me when the colors dancing across the sky reflect off the stone. Lifting her hand, I press a kiss to her finger above the ring before tugging her back into my arms.

"Merry Christmas, princess."

I don't let her respond, just slide my mouth over hers, my tongue dueling with hers as the sky shifts above our heads.

The rest of what we do that night isn't fit to tell Santa. But we definitely solidify our permanent residence on the naughty list.

I've never been happier to claim my coal or help the woman of my dreams claim hers.

THE END

LOVE EVAN & LILAH? If swoony rock stars are your kryptonite, how about one who is also a single dad? Keep reading for a sneak peek of their bandmate's single dad/nanny, age gap, happily ever after!

FALLING FOR THE BEAT

CHRIS

"*G*od dammit."

The phone ringing for the second time in as many minutes distracts me from the chord progression I'm working through. I need to finish this song since it's been partially done for months. But finishing will have to wait—again. With a sigh, I drop the pick and snag my phone from the table.

"Hello?"

"Chris?" Frank Nguyen has been my attorney since I was old enough to need one. And since he was my parents' attorney first, he's been a fixture in my life for a lot longer than that.

"Frank. How's it going?" I set the guitar aside and lean back against the couch.

"I want to say fine, but I just got the strangest phone call. From an attorney named Nathaniel Ramirez."

Fuck.

I should have known. I massage the bridge of my nose where a headache is now taking root.

"Which band member is being sued for paternity now?"

On the surface, it sounds like a strange question. But with the number of times Milo, Finn, or Noah have been accused of fathering a child, it's one I ask far more than I ever thought I would.

For over twenty years, we had more than our fair share of women claiming that one of us had fathered her child. Miraculously, none of the accusations had ever been legitimate. But our luck wouldn't hold out forever. And as the leader of our band, it's my job to handle this. *They* are my responsibility.

Thank fuck Evan is too quiet to cause this kind of shit. I'd bet money Frank is calling me about Milo, since our drummer has chased more pussy than the rest of us combined.

"Er, it's not that. Not really."

"Not really?" Surging off the couch, I walk the length of my music room without finding the comfort it usually brings me.

"Does the name Melanie Sanders mean anything to you?"

I freeze mid-stride and take a breath. Melanie and I met almost seven years ago at a party here in LA. Her friend had somehow scored invitations. The friend had been swooped up by Finn, and I swooped in on Mel, who leaned against a wall seeming more than a little out of place. She had looked at me with those big hazel eyes like I was some kind of savior.

More like Lucifer.

I wasn't her Mr. Right. But our on-again, off-again fling had lasted two years before she broke it off completely when she wanted the monogamy I couldn't give her. But I wasn't overly heartbroken. With the constant tours, I was rarely in LA, and even when I was, we were in the studio recording the next album. I never expected her to wait around for me.

No way was Frank calling me about a paternity issue

there. Melanie had my number. And the last time I slept with her had been almost six years ago.

"Melanie? What about her?"

"She's dead."

What the fuck?

I pull the phone away from my ear, staring at it like it will somehow tell me the truth.

"She was thirty-two." As if her age is some sort of protection.

"Car accident." He clears his throat in the awkward silence. "Nathaniel Ramirez is the probate attorney in charge of Melanie's estate."

I'm still struggling to process that Mel is dead. Probate? Estate?

"What? Why did he reach out to you?"

"Chris, Melanie named you in her will as the father of her four-year-old son, Gage Christopher Rivera. She identified you as his guardian in the event that something should happen to her."

I'm overwhelmed by dizziness and reach blindly for a wall, leaning against it as I take several breaths. That first night, Melanie knew me as Topher Rivers, my stage name. But it didn't take long before I tired of her calling out another man's name in bed. So I confided in her and gave her my real name—Christopher Antonio Rivera.

"Son?" I gasp.

I have a son. A four-year-old. Gage. One corner of my mouth quirks at the unique name that reminds me of Mel. She may have seemed like a conservative, librarian type, but she had a wild streak she showed to very few people.

"I already requested that Nathaniel initiate a paternity test—"

"He's mine." I don't need a fucking test.

Mel wouldn't name me as the father otherwise.

"Chris." The lecture is obvious in Frank's tone.

"Frank. I don't doubt he's mine."

"I know you want to believe that. But it would be better to confirm it."

"I don't need a fucking test." My molars click together. Why isn't he listening to me?

"Think about it from the child's—"

"Gage."

Frank sighs. "Gage's perspective. He's already lost his mother. We need to be sure before we upend his life again."

Fuck. I didn't think about that.

"Where is he now?"

I don't care what Frank thinks. If Gage is in foster care, I won't hesitate to go pick him up. No child deserves to lose his mother and his home all in one day.

"Melanie's parents have temporary custody."

I never met her parents. But the stories she told me assure me that my son is okay with them for the time being.

"Find somewhere quick, Frank. I want this test over and done with and the results confirmed."

As soon as we hang up, I send a text to the guys.

> Congratulations, you're all uncles.

Four weeks. A month since Frank called to tell me I have a son. But finally, the results are in, and Gage's grandparents can't postpone anymore. They have—twice. But today is the day.

It's been a long four weeks. Once I told Mamá and Papá that they were grandparents—again—I had to beg them to not immediately rush to the Sanderses and meet their new grandson. Fuck, I still hadn't met him.

"This is bullshit," I mutter quietly, but loud enough for Evan to hear me.

"Don't worry. I'll make everyone clear out once they get here."

He and the rest of the guys showed up this morning, despite knowing that the Sanderses are dropping Gage off any minute now.

"What?"

"The guys. I'll get everyone to clear out when they get here." Evan glances up at me from the pool lounger he's kicked back on while Milo and Finn take turns cannon-balling into my pool. Noah is on another chair, dark glasses concealing most of his face and a silver flask glinting in the sun where it presses against his lips.

"I know. I figured that. I just can't believe it's taken a fucking month."

I gesture to Noah, and Evan fixes his attention on our keyboardist. His shoulders tighten despite the heavy sigh he exhales.

"Shit. I'll take him home with me. Make sure he stays out of trouble."

"We need to record the new album. Cornerstone is already breathing fire since it's taken this long. We can't afford for him to go to rehab."

Again.

I don't say it, but I don't need to.

In the last three years, Noah's had three separate stints in rehab. It's been hell on our schedule, and we've barely kept our touring commitments, forget recording anything new.

My phone chimes with a notification from the guard at the gate.

"They're on their way." My heart gallops in my chest and my palms grow clammy. I'm amazed the phone doesn't slide out of my grip.

"All right, boys, that's the signal. Time to go. Milo, Finn, dry off. No way am I letting you in my car soaking wet."

They grumble but grab towels from the outdoor chest before following a surly Noah and a silent Evan to the front door. I bring up the rear, rolling my eyes at the trail of water they leave behind. The guys are barely in Evan's car when another one pulls up behind them.

I was expecting two adults. Instead, three meet me at the front door while Gage hides behind the woman.

"Mr. Rivera?" The man dressed in a suit steps forward with his hand extended. "I'm the Sanderses' attorney, Stephen Chen."

"Attorney?" I shake his hand distractedly. "Do I need to call Frank?"

"Mr. Nguyen? That won't be necessary. I'm here at the request of my clients to ensure the transfer goes smoothly."

I bite back the attitude I want to sling at his smarmy little speech. My son is watching.

"I don't anticipate any issues."

"It shouldn't have to happen at all." If looks could kill, the one Mrs. Sanders shoots my direction would have me six feet under.

"Excuse me?" I turn my attention from the attorney to her.

"He doesn't even know you. Who do you think you are to take our last piece of Melanie away from us?"

"Is that what you think I'm doing?" Her words are sucker punches to my gut. I didn't choose for Melanie to list me as guardian. But if she hadn't, I would have never known about Gage.

"He loves us. He's used to us." Mr. Sanders takes up where his wife left off.

"Mr. Sanders. Mrs. Sanders. I'm terribly sorry for your loss. But I can't be sorry about meeting my son. I don't want to take him from you. I *want* you to have a relationship with him."

Mr. Sanders opens his mouth to reply, but the attorney cuts him off.

"Tom, Bethany." He shakes his head, and I want to know what the fuck he's thinking.

The two other adults say nothing else. I'm missing something here. What the fuck does it take for their attorney to only say their names to shut them up?

"Gage," the lawyer addresses my son and snaps his fingers. "Come here."

My hands clench into fists at my side.

Stay the fuck away from my son.

The little boy steps forward, moving out from behind his grandmother's legs. Light brown hair falls across his forehead, and I can't help but trace the similar fall of my hair. Wide hazel eyes remind me of Mel, and his cheeks still show the baby he used to be—the apples dusted pink while small lips purse together as he studies me.

He lets go of his grandma's hand. She gasps and keeps her arm extended awkwardly in the air, like she's ready to snatch him away from me, even though she has no reason—and no right—to do so.

"Does he know who I am?" He approaches me slowly, and I hold my breath.

"We told him we were bringing him to meet his father." The attorney's voice grates against my ears. I can't wait for him to leave.

Gage now stands directly in front of me, and I lower to my haunches and smile at him.

"Hi, buddy."

"Hi."

"Do you know who I am?"

His little head bobs once. "Daddy."

Tears burn behind my eyes, and I blink several times to clear the sensation.

Fuck.

I'm a goner.

I've fallen in love with a kid I just met. No, not simply any kid. My son.

I don't regret my life as a rock star, but for the first time in thirty-six years, I can see the appeal of being a family man.

"That's right, Gage. I'm your daddy."

At that, he steps forward, and his little arms wrap around my neck. I inhale his strawberry and little boy scent. Mrs. Sanders sniffles, and the attorney clears his throat.

"Tom, Gage's bags?"

Mrs. Sanders follows her husband to the car, but she gets in while he and the attorney grab two suitcases and two boxes—one labeled "Books" and one labeled "Toys"—and set them by the porch.

"That's everything."

Mr. Sanders looks at me and then at Gage before waving half-heartedly and joining his wife in the car. The attorney is the last to get in, and I don't relax until his door closes behind him.

"Daddy?"

My attention shifts from the departing car to the little boy standing next to me.

"Yeah, bud?"

"I have to go potty."

"Okay. Let's go potty."

I got this.

I don't got this.

By the end of the first month, even with the help of Lois, my part-time housekeeper, who increased her hours to help, I'm still floundering. I'm practically catatonic from lack of sleep. Every night this week, Gage has either woken up with nightmares, had an accident, or climbed into bed with me for no reason. I had no idea such a small human could take up so much room on a king-size bed, but inevitably, his little foot digs into my kidney whenever he falls asleep.

"Why don't you find a nanny?" Evan asks. He showed up after Gage was asleep so we could work on song selections for the next album.

"I asked my mom to help me find one. Anytime I try to do it, I'm yanked back into band shit."

Band shit. Noah high as fuck last weekend. Milo and Finn whoring and partying it up all over town.

"Are you still meeting with Jax and Nick?"

The co-owners of Arrhythmic Records reached out to me about a song I wrote that Just One Yesterday wouldn't record —not our sound. But it's perfect for one of their artists, Dylan Graves, and they want me to work with him on the song.

"Yeah. I managed to eke out some time tomorrow afternoon." Trying to add that to my already chaotic schedule has proved almost impossible. It's the weekend, but neither of them balked when I suggested it.

"What about Gage?"

"Mamá." One word, but it's explanation enough.

"He hasn't said anything in days?"

Over the last month, Gage has become less and less talkative. He's gone from a vibrant little boy to a quiet shell of himself. He hasn't uttered a single word since breakfast two days ago when he asked for waffles like he used to have with Mommy. Only I had no idea what kind of waffles she made for him. Apparently, they were Eggos, like the ones in my freezer. But I didn't know.

I didn't understand.

I'm failing. Otherwise, my son would still be speaking.

"No." Sighing, I flop down on the couch next to Evan and run my hands through my hair.

"What's your mom say?"

"She said I need to take him to a therapist. That it's probably his way of grieving."

"You gonna do it?"

Having known Evan since junior high, I ignore his usual snarky tone.

"I need to find someone first."

"Sounds like a lot of work."

"Yeah." And all I want to do is fucking sleep.

But there's no rest for the weary. Or the wicked. And I definitely fall into both categories.

What happens when the woman Chris hires to help is one he can't resist falling for? You can binge Falling for the Beat in KU!

Polish your jingle bells, strategically hang the mistletoe, and get ready to claim your spot on The Naughty List. This holiday season, fourteen of your favorite authors are spicing up the cocoa and taking advantage of those long winter nights, proving that sometimes it's more fun to claim your coal than it is to stay on Santa's good side. After all, well-behaved women might make the nice list, but naughty ones have all the fun...

Grab the Whole Series here: https://geni.us/TheNaughtyListSeries

PLAYLIST

You would think that writing a Christmas novel would mean tons of Christmas carols, right? Blame too many years in retail while I was in high school and college because I just couldn't (if I did, it would probably sound more like Trans-Siberian Orchestra than traditional Christmas carols). But there are some really good songs that embody that push/pull of Evan and Lilah's relationship. "Closer" by Boyce Avenue and Sarah Hyland mixes with "In the Air Tonight" by State of Mine and "Blinding Lights" by Saint Asonia.

Want to hear the full playlist? Check out the playlist on Spotify by searching for the "Rockin' Around the Christmas Tree" playlist or scan the QR code below.

 You can find all the my playlists on my website:
https://www.breannalynnau
thor.com

ACKNOWLEDGMENTS

THANK YOU! YES, YOU! It was almost three years ago when I started thinking I could actually write and publish the stories that existed in my head. Some of you found me at the beginning with Jax and Charlie and some of you are just meeting Evan and Lilah, two band members of Just One Yesterday. I hope you enjoyed reading this story as much as I did writing it!

MY FAMILY—thank you for supporting me in this dream. For asking for a signed paperback, for sharing my work with others, for your love. I couldn't have done this without you! I love you!

DENNIS—for helping me learn that I still have more chapters in my story, for holding my hand and beginning our journey.

CLAIRE & ALINA—there are not enough words to tell you both how grateful I am to have you in my life.

BETH—I can't imagine not having all our weekly conversations. I had a blast in Makinac and look forward to our next retreat!

TO THE OTHER NAUGHTY LIST AUTHORS—I was so excited to be a part of this! Thank you for being awesome!

TO EVERYONE WHO HELPED ME CREATE, MOLD, AND POLISH ROCKIN' AROUND THE CHRISTMAS TREE INTO WHAT IT IS— THANK YOU, THANK YOU, THANK YOU!

ALSO BY BREANNA LYNN

ABOUT THE AUTHOR

Breanna Lynn lives in Colorado with her two sets of twins (affectionately referred to as the Twinx), her boyfriend, his son, their two dogs, and three cats. A classy connoisseur of all things coffee, Breanna spends her free time keeping the Twinx from taking over the world. When not coordinating chaos, Breanna can be found binge reading, listening to music, or watching rom-coms with a giant bowl of popcorn.

Want to follow Breanna? Scan the QR code for all the ways to stay caught up!

www.ingramcontent.com/pod-product-compliance
Lightning Source LLC
Chambersburg PA
CBHW072028170626
46811CB00008B/2982